Don't miss Barry J. Farber's previous books

DIAMONDS UNDER PRESSURE

"Barry Farber provides a practical and solid road map for success and shows us how today's adversities and obstacles can be turned into challenges for tomorrow."

—John Gray

DIAMOND IN THE ROUGH

"A tour de force on how to think . . . A MUST-READING for every grade school, high school, and college student. There ought to be courses based on this book in every institution of learning in the country. Then students would learn the things in life that are really important. Your book is a road map!"

—Richard J. Waller, vice-president, TeleRap

"This is destined to be a classic on personal success, however you define it. This book is full of powerful, practical, and remarkably simple ideas that anyone can use immediately to improve any part of their life. I read it in one sitting."

—Brian Tracy, Brian Tracy International

"Barry J. Farber's book *Diamond in the Rough* is a welcome change! Barry gives practical common sense ideas about achieving success. In fact, I strongly believe every high school kid should read Barry's book before they graduate or enter the workforce!"

—Rich R. Ragnanese, WERE Talk Radio

What people are saying about Barry Farber . . .

"Barry's powerful and practical ideas come from his achievements in the real world of sales and business success. He's made a huge contribution to our national sales force!"

—Joe Bourdow, president, Val-Pak

"Barry Farber's program is the best mental training you can get!"

—Bruce Jenner, Olympic Gold Medalist

"We all very much enjoyed your presentation and certainly your humor, as demonstrated by the standing ovation. Many expressed to me personally how much they enjoyed your stories, thoughts and perspective of F.O.C.U.S."

—Bill Golliher, Anderson News Company

"The highest rated speaker at our conference."

—*Inc.* magazine

"I always thought 'knock your socks off' was a figure of speech. Until, that is, you addressed our group."

—Richard H. Schneeberg, president and CEO, The Consortium

"Great program! You were a big hit among both the sales reps, as well as sales management."

—Charles Steele, Great-West Life

DIVE
RIGHT
IN

DIVE RIGHT IN

101 Powerful
Action Steps
for Personal
Achievement

BARRY J. FARBER

BERKLEY BOOKS, NEW YORK

DIVE RIGHT IN

A Berkley Book/ published by arrangement with
the author

PRINTING HISTORY
Berkley trade paperback edition/September 1999

The Penguin Putnam Inc. World Wide Web site address is
http://www.penguinputnam.com

ISBN: 0-425-17042-X

BERKLEY ®
Berkley Books are published by The Berkley Publishing Group,
a division of Penguin Putnam Inc.,
375 Hudson Street, New York, New York 10014.
BERKLEY and the "B" design are trademarks belonging to Penguin Putnam Inc.

PRINTED IN THE UNITED STATES OF AMERICA

10 9 8 7 6 5 4 3 2 1

DEDICATED TO MY FAMILY:
ALLISON, HALLIE, JORDAN, AND SAM.

ACKNOWLEDGEMENTS

Special thanks to the following people who make my life a whole lot easier: Sharyn Kolberg, Tony Wainwright, George Hiltzik, Al Zuckerman, and Hillary Cige.

CONTENTS

Introduction   xiii

1 Action Steps for
   LEARNING   1

2 Action Steps for
   PLANNING   33

3 Action Steps for
   EFFORT   75

4 Action Steps for
   ADDING VALUE   111

5 Action Steps for
   ENERGY   131

6 Action Steps for
   MARKETING YOURSELF   155

7 Action Steps for
   OVERCOMING OBSTACLES   167

INTRODUCTION

A Zen student and master stood by the edge of a rushing stream. The student said, "Master, I cannot learn this lesson. I do not understand." The master did not reply. Instead, he pushed the student into the stream and held his head underneath the water. One minute went by, then two. The student began to struggle. His arms flailing all around, the student pushed up against the master's hand as hard as he could. Finally, the master let go of the student's head.

The student gasped for air and then said, "Master, why did you do that?"

The master replied, "When you want to learn as badly as you wanted to take that breath, you will find the answer."

Over the years, people have often said to me, "After all the things you've done and all the people you've worked with, what do you think are the keys to personal achievement?" I have given many different answers to that question as my perspective was evolving and changing. Sometimes I would say attitude, sometimes I would answer honesty. There were times when I said understanding failure was the key to personal achievement, or focusing on service, or being persistent.

But when I heard the story of the Zen student and master, I knew I had found the answer. We all have deficiencies and areas of weakness. There will always be people who have more skills and maybe even more talent than we do. But when you are as hungry for something as that student was for air, when you have that passion inside you, when you believe so much in what you want to accomplish, you can overcome any obstacles that may appear in front of you. And when you are fueled by that hunger and passion, there's only one thing you can do: *take action.*

If you're hungry and you do nothing about it, you will surely starve. You must take action to relieve that hunger. If you have dreams and do nothing about them, you will face spiritual starvation. You must take action to turn your dreams into achievable goals.

Taking action is what this book is about. This is actually the third in a series of books about personal achievement. The first book, *Diamond in the Rough*, is about discovering and mining the potential within each of us, and learning to use that potential to achieve success. The second book, *Diamonds Under Pressure*, is about adversity—what to do when "bad" things happen, when obstacles get in your way, when failure strikes you down and you think you may never get up again. Both of these are incredibly important lessons to learn.

Diamond in the Rough talks a lot about how we think about ourselves, our friends, and family, and about our attitudes toward success. High achievers believe that the right attitude usually means the difference between success and failure. Successful people expect things to turn out well and have every confidence in their own abilities to make things happen.

While I was writing that book, however, I discovered something else about successful people. No matter how much success you achieve, no matter how far you go, you'll never follow a straight and narrow path from rags to riches, from bottom to top. It is guaranteed that at some point in your life, you will experience failure. You will run into adversity, challenges, setbacks, conflicts, stress, rejection, disappointment, defeat, and frustration. The higher you reach, the farther you are likely to fall. It happens to everyone.

Based upon the fact that success and adversity go hand in hand, I wanted to write something about how to cope with setbacks and failures, and how to use them to move us forward. That led to *Diamonds Under Pressure*. What is it that enables people to get past the failure and move on to success? It's the ability to learn from failure and disappointment, to be energized by rejection, not defeated by it. It's the willingness to look at an obstacle as a challenge, almost to dare yourself: "Let's see how you deal with this one!" Successful people get discouraged and depressed just like everyone else, but they don't wallow in it. They get right back up, strengthen their resolve, and start over again.

This is what led me to think about writing this book, the third in a logical sequence for building the foundation for success:

- **First, believe in yourself.** Know that your dreams are important, that you have the potential to do what you want. In fact, you have the potential to go beyond what you might dream possible.

- **Second, know that failure comes with the territory.** It's something that everyone experiences. Great athletes have lost games. Oscar-winning actors have appeared in flops. Billionaires have come back from bankruptcy. Brilliant scientists have made important discoveries only after understanding why most of their experiments didn't work. It's not the failure that counts, it's what you learn from it.

- **Third, take action.** Most of the time, it's not what we do that we regret. It's what we never did, the road not taken, the missed opportunity. Listen the next time you hear someone say, "I wish I had done this. . . ." or "If only I had done that. . . ." You can hear the sadness and the sense of loss in his or her voice. Listen, too, to a person who has attempted a difficult task and did not succeed. When he says, "Well, at least I tried!" there is pride in his voice. There is a feeling of accomplishment, even if the outcome wasn't all he desired.

The rest of this book is about taking action—not just any action, but action that has thought and depth behind it. It's about taking qualified action. It's not enough just to take a step—you could walk off a cliff. It's taking a step in the right direction with the right information. This book will allow you to focus on all types of action in a variety of circumstances and situations.

In everyday life, we all move forward by taking one step at a time. No matter what occupation we hold—advertising executive, actor, entrepreneur, secretary, corporate manager, lawyer, astronaut, sales representative—our biggest challenge is to take that first step into unknown, uncharted territory. And, for many of us, that first step is always the hardest.

Perhaps we let the fear of failure block our way, or we hesitate because we don't have a clear purpose in mind. Perhaps we're not comfortable with the people we're approaching, or the situation in which we find ourselves. This book is designed to help any person, in any profession or lifestyle, who is hesitant to try new things: hesitant to ask for an interview; to ask for a date; to ask for a raise; or to ask someone for help. It's designed for anyone who ever wished they could just get up the nerve, and get up the energy, to turn their boldest dreams and desires into focused, practical, result-oriented *action*.

The strategies outlined here provide the tools and techniques necessary to eliminate apathy, lethargy, and the reluctance to move ahead. This book will help you get more out of life (professionally and personally) by taking those action steps that make a difference to your life. These strategies can help you understand what is really blocking you from moving forward.

Start the book anywhere. Of course, you can read the book from beginning to end. If, however, you're pressed for time (and/or are looking for some instant gratification), just open the book to any page and use that action step as your plan for the day. Or, choose one of the seven categories of action and read that section all at once. It doesn't matter how you do it. In fact, the action steps are meant to be read again and again—and applied.

There is no substitute for experience. I can't take the action for you. I can tell you what works for me and for others who have given me their words of wisdom, but the only way you'll know if these action steps work for you is to go out and try them.

It's easy to say, "Take action." But if it were that easy to do, we'd all be at the pinnacle of success. Taking action—focused, smart, creative action—may seem the most basic of all skills, but it is often the biggest challenge that companies, and individuals, face: the reluctance to make that call, to make a decision, to take one step forward. That's all it takes—one step forward at a time—but it's taking that first step that often keeps people from attaining the success they desire.

Dive Right In is designed to help you take that first step, and to cross the fine line that fear creates to inhibit us from moving forward. If we don't take those early steps, the fine line becomes an ever-thickening barrier. And once we've taken those first steps, we have to commit ourselves to making a continued effort to generate energy and activity. It is this constant generation of activity that will put the odds in our favor and keep us always moving toward our dreams.

The action steps included here serve as a reminder that what we see when we look at high achievers is the dramatic result of mundane, yet necessary, action. We see the end result; we don't see all the hard work that has gone before. We often assume some element of luck was involved. Success in life is never achieved through luck. Sure, there are the few exceptions, people who were "discovered" simply walking down the street, or who have been handed opportunities on a silver platter. These people may have had a head start in life, but even those lucky few have had to work hard to maintain what they were given.

The Oscar-winning actress Kathy Bates was a guest on a television interview program one night, talking about how success had come to her relatively late in life. Although she had been a hardworking Broadway actress for many years, she saw the film versions of many parts she played on stage go to more glamorous Hollywood stars. Her role in Stephen King's *Misery* changed all that. Now she is herself a recognized Hollywood star. The interviewer asked her if there was a difference in her work now that she was such a success. "No, the work is the same," Bates answered quickly. "Success is the cherry on the cake. You've still got to bake the cake every day."

ACTION STEPS FOR LEARNING

THE purpose of this book is not only to help you take action, but to help you evaluate the most efficient, most valuable methods of taking action. This section focuses on the steps you take before you take a step. How to make the best possible move in the shortest period of time. Since this is a book about action, it's my duty to remind you that you don't need to stop what you're doing to gain knowledge. Of course you learn from study and observation, but you learn most from doing.

Knowledge should be a foundation for action, not a barrier to it. Action and learning go hand in hand. Remember, every action you take provides a lesson for the next.

1

Applying everything you know will return more value than everything you've learned.

If there is one great philosophy in life, it is this: Learn something new every day. Learning is one of the greatest investments you will ever make in yourself. But—and this is a big one—learning is useless if it is not followed by action and application. Learning is not an end unto itself; it is a means to an end.

There are people who become known as perpetual students. They stay in school forever and gather many degrees. But they actually accomplish very little. There are other people who never get beyond grade school and who become great successes in their lives. So it is not the *formal* learning that makes the difference. Perpetual students may have brains crammed full of obscure facts, but they are not serving themselves or those around them. They are no more than a storage facility for knowledge. Those people who do not learn much in school often make up for it in other ways. They get their education from everything they experience—and they constantly apply those lessons to their lives. They increase the value of their knowledge exponentially by taking the actions that enable them to keep growing and achieving.

We have to understand that the world can only be grasped by action, not by contemplation. The hand is more important than the eye. . . . The hand is the cutting edge of the mind.

JACOB BRONOWSKI

Before you take any action, educate yourself.

THIS book is about taking action—not just any action, but action that has thought and depth behind it. Effective action is based on knowledge, and that knowledge comes from many sources. It can come from reference sources such as books, audiotapes, and the Internet; it can come from your own personal experiences; and it can come from the advice and insights of people who have experience in your area of interest. After you have gathered all the information you can, synthesize what you've learned and adapt it to your own needs and abilities.

You don't ask for advice so that you can do exactly what another person has done. That would be cheating yourself, leaving your own ideas and talents out of the equation. You're getting advice in order to gather input and make your actions strong and effective.

The need to educate yourself doesn't stop just because you've attained a certain level of success. Joe Bourdow is president of Val-Pak, the largest local cooperative direct mail company in the world. You know those blue envelopes you get in the mail with coupons from local businesses? That's Bourdow's company. Bourdow started his career in college as a radio newsman, and his job was to go out and get the story. And although he is now president of a large company and in charge of twenty-five hundred people, he still feels that's his job.

"I'm confronted with problems every day, and I pretend I'm a reporter and I'm trying to get the story right," he says. "I'm trying to understand what the headline is and what the lead is. I'm trying to understand all of the issues and get the facts from the various sources. When I get to the point in a particular problem or issue where I feel I can write the story, then chances are I can make the story come out however I want it to. It helps me make a decision and then communicate that decision to the organization."

Bourdow tackles most problems as if he were an outside reporter with no previous knowledge of the subject. "Many times I don't know anything," he says. "We're putting in twelve million dollars' worth of computers here. Aside from messing around on the Internet, I am by no means a techie. But by asking questions and reading and doing research just as if I were working on a story, I'm able to get to a point where I can make a decision."

That is the whole purpose of education—so that you can make smart, well-thought-out decisions, which lead to efficient, effective actions.

After you take any action, reeducate yourself.

As soon as you've completed an action step, it's time to step back and take an objective look at it. If it was performed perfectly, then you should know how it was accomplished so that you can repeat the process. If all did not go as planned, however, you need to get feedback about what you did wrong, and how you can improve for the next time.

This feedback can come from both yourself and others. If you're able to identify what you did wrong, you can make plans for improvement. Perhaps you just need more practice and/or experience. Perhaps you did not plan well enough, or did not do enough research beforehand. It's important to retrace your steps, figure out what went wrong and why, and find ways to make the next steps more positive.

It's not always easy to be objective about yourself or your work. There are times when you're not sure exactly why you failed, or why things did not go as well as you had hoped. That's when it's good to get feedback from others you trust. They may be able to give you a better understanding of how to make your next actions stronger and more effective.

For the best feedback, call on a minimum of three people. Tell them: "This is what I did, this is what happened, what would you do next?" The three people you call should have different backgrounds, different experiences, and different viewpoints. Then you study the three suggestions you've gathered and choose the one (or ones) that make the most sense for you. That feedback, plus your own evaluation of the situation, will provide you with a strong foundation to move on to the next step and to increase your chances of success the next time around.

4

Experiment with your life.

You have one life; you have one chance to do as much as you can and reach your highest potential. The only way you can discover that potential is to experiment and experience, to use your mind and body fully, to engage yourself totally in life. You are a perfect instrument for testing what you see, hear, feel, smell, and touch. The more you engage your senses, the more you can experience and understand the world around you. Ask yourself, "What is the truth of this experience?"

Last year I decided I wanted to take up a musical instrument. Someone told me that the violin was the most unforgiving instrument, and I decided to take up the challenge. I was trying to learn vibrato. Several people told me not even to try, that I would have to play for a long time before I learned that skill. But then one man, Richard Menzel, one of the most highly respected masters of violin making and repair in the country, agreed to teach me how to do it. First, he said, he would have to actually take my finger and physically move it for me. Since it was something I had never done before, the brain had no way of giving the muscles the necessary instructions. Once he moved my finger for me, my brain had the instructions it needed, and I could do it myself.

That was a great lesson for me. It taught me much more than vibrato. It taught me that everything you do adds dimension and elasticity to the brain. You never stop learning. We often confuse "I don't know how to do that" with "I could never do that." We don't know what we can or cannot do until we try. Some tasks will be difficult until the brain gets the right set of instructions to give to the muscles.

There may be times when you experiment with something and it doesn't work out. You might find you hate it. That's okay, that's part of life. Everything you try expands your brain power that much more. The information you absorb from each thing you attempt gets passed on to the next thing you try. So the most important concept you can ever grasp is this: It's not whether you succeed at each thing you attempt, but that you continue to make the attempts that matters.

The only way to experiment is through action—to fail, to fall, to rise up and try again. I believe that we are all put here for a reason. We all have deficiencies, but God does not make junk. Knowing that forces me to put myself to the test, to push my limits further and further, using my entire body and mind. I want to reach that place of confidence, that solid ground of understanding that only comes through when we have put forth our very best efforts.

Our own life is the instrument with which we experiment with truth.

THICH NHAT HANH

5

Always begin with an open mind.

THERE are times when knowing nothing about a subject, being an absolute beginner, has a definite advantage. When you become an "expert" at something, you get set in your ways. It's difficult to learn new techniques, or to be open to creative suggestions. It's easier just to follow the old worn path.

The beginner has no path to follow. He must make his own way, make his own mistakes, and forge his own successes. The expert sees the limits; the beginner sees the possibilities. Every action we take should be a rebirth. Don't forget the lessons you've learned from experience, but don't shut out that seeking, searching, curious child's mind that's amazed by every new turn in the road.

In the beginner's mind there are many possibilities, but in the expert's mind there are few.

SHUNRYU SUZUKI

Learn the foundations of your profession.

YEARS ago, schools used to teach the Palmer method of writing. It taught three basic loops from which any letter of the alphabet could be formed. Once you learned those three loops, learning script was easy.

The same applies in everything you do. There are basic foundations you need to know so you can build your skills upon them. If you're learning to play the violin, you must start by learning the finger positions and the bowing techniques that apply whether you're playing elementary scales or a complicated symphony. If you're starting a new business, you must learn the fundamentals of your industry upon which you will erect your success.

Once you have mastered the fundamentals, you continue to learn. Albert Einstein's greatest frustration in life was that no matter how deep he dug, no matter how much he studied, he could never come up with a definitive answer. There was always more to be discovered. This may be frustrating, but it's also exciting. It means that there are endless possibilities in the world. Instead of questioning why things are so complex, rejoice in the fact that there's no end to what you can learn.

Rejoice also in the fact that the studying and learning you do in one area is transferable to every other area of your life. You learn more than facts and skills—you learn how to learn. The same methods you use to absorb the fundamentals of the violin can be used to learn anything else. The goal is to be able to apply the knowledge you gain to your own situation and personal reality. Knowledge is wasted if it is not used to benefit yourself and others.

Vincent van Gogh once wrote: "If you study Japanese art, you see a man who is undoubtedly wise, philosophic, and intelligent, who spends his time how? In studying the distance between the earth and the moon? No. In studying the policy of Bismarck? No. He studies a single blade of grass. But his blade of grass leads him to draw every plant and then the seasons, the wide aspects of the countryside, then animals, then the human figure. So he passes his life, and life is too short to do the whole."

The point is not that you paint the same blade of grass over and over again. The point is that by learning the art of painting the grass, you learn the whole art of painting; by learning the whole art of painting, you learn the process of learning; by learning the process of learning, you can learn everything else in the world.

7

Focus on your craft with such depth and passion that confidence slices through like a knife through butter.

Here is a winning combination that will never let you down: Knowledge + belief = confidence. When you know everything there is to know about your craft or your product or your business or your project, and you believe in it so much that nothing can shake your faith, the result is confidence. And that confidence will get you through more obstacles than anything else.

Confidence is built on the foundation of learning as much as you can about what you're trying to do, and by believing in yourself and your abilities. When you have this kind of confidence, people have confidence in you. They just assume that you know what you're doing, and that you can achieve whatever you set out to do. When your confidence level is at its peak, you can push through obstacles that would have seemed impassable before.

Confidence comes when you take pride in yourself and what you do. That is not to be confused with being cocky or boastful. Bob Parisi is vice president of Southern Business Operations for Roche Laboratories. He played football in college. He remembers the time a defensive-back coach told him, "You've got to believe that no one can get behind you to the goal line. Because if they do, they'll score a touchdown and you'll feel terrible. As long as you believe that no one will get behind you, they probably won't." The only way you get confidence is if you're prepared, you're knowledgeable, and you're skillful. If you're deficient in any of those three things, you can begin to doubt yourself. And when doubt sets in, you'll begin to believe that someone can get behind you.

8

The key to success is knowing what you have to know.

Bob Parisi has been with Roche Laboratories for over thirty years, and he knows what it takes for people within his company to be successful.

"No matter what business you're in, or what you're trying to accomplish, there are certain skills and competencies that are necessary in order to be successful," he says. "One of the greatest keys to success is the ability to recognize and understand what those skills are. And you have to be able to practice them often."

This is something Parisi knows from his own experience. When he first started out at Roche as a sales representative, his division manager said, "In five years, you should no longer be a sales rep. You should be looking for positions of greater responsibility."

"That's great," Parisi replied. "But what is it going to take to get there? What do I have to do to be qualified to vie for a position of greater responsibility?"

The manager's answer? "Get really good at what you do. Gain recognition for what you do. In other words, become as knowledgeable as you can, and develop the skills and competencies of your job." He advised Parisi to set goals for himself, to map out exactly the kinds of things he wanted to accomplish. Then to go out and do them.

"You have to have a plan," says Parisi. "And you have to learn as much about the new job as possible. Suppose you want to be a manager. You can get books on management. You may be able to get into a management training program. You can observe your own manager, work with him for a few days to find out what skills you need to be a good manager. As long as you have a plan, and you keep working toward that plan, you'll be surprised at how quickly you can accomplish all the things you need to get to the next position."

It all comes from within, from a sense of urgency and a will to win. You must have pride in accomplishing a certain level of mastery in whatever it is you do, whether you're a baker or a professional athlete or a businessperson. You can't be run of the mill; you have to be really good at what you do.

"It takes a lot of hard work," says Parisi. "There are an awful lot of disappointments. You have to be ready to accept the word 'no'. You need to have a tremendous amount of intestinal fortitude and tenacity."

9

When you think you have learned everything, learn more.

THE most successful people in every field know that they can never fully master their craft. There is always something new to learn. It's when we think we know it all that we get stuck in those famous ruts and find it difficult to move forward. Life does not come in a neat little package tied up in a bow. There is never a time when you can say, "Ah, now I know everything about this subject."

One man who is a perfect example of continuous learning is master violin maker Richard Menzel. He spent more than thirty years as an engineer at the Lockheed Corporation. Yet he always made time for his love of music. He played the violin and studied it from both a musical and an engineering point of view. When he left Lockheed to open his shop, he continued his quest for knowledge.

Menzel studies every aspect of his business. He uses the standard tools of his trade, but he often creates the tools to fix those tools. And he invents new tools to study areas of violin engineering no one else has explored. He created an instrument to measure the angle of your arm when you're moving the bow from string to string so that you can gauge and improve your form. He invented a machine to study the properties of the horsehair used in making bows. "The bow is just a stick with some hair on it," he says. "The challenge is to take less and make more out of it. How much pressure does it take to break this hair? Nobody knows. How much does it stretch? How much does it expand over time? Nobody knows, but I want to find out."

He has invented a tool to measure the amount of pressure it takes to bring a string down to make contact with the wood. Ideally, he could use that knowledge to construct a violin that would take equal pressure all along the length of the string, which would make a better sound. Such a violin may be impossible to construct, but Menzel continues his study with the hope that someday he will find the solution.

In fact, he admits frustration at the lack of closure in his learning.

"There is no end to studying," he says. "When you solve one problem, it just leads to other questions to be answered." But it is the pursuit of those answers that give us energy and enthusiasm for life, that makes us look forward to endless possibilities that lie ahead. To say "I have learned enough" is to stop living.

Wisdom is like a mass of fire—it cannot be entered from any side. Wisdom is like a clear pool—it can be entered from any side.

NAGARJUNA

10

Motivate yourself with the power of music.

In a quiet bedroom somewhere in America, a pregnant woman sits in a chair, slowly rocking back and forth. She is holding a portable cassette player and inserts a tape of Mozart sonatas, her favorite music. She is careful to place the headphone just right to get the best sound—not over her ears, but onto her abdomen so that her unborn baby can hear. Over the past several decades, many studies have shown that music stimulates both physical movement and emotional well-being in unborn and newborn babies. (Of course, every parent who has ever sung a child a lullaby knew that already.)

The power of music is not just limited to babies. Researchers at the Music School in Providence, Rhode Island, recently found that music students usually perform better on standardized math tests than other students. And, according to Dr. Arthur Winter in his book, *Brain Workout*, music is a highly effective tool to improve your brain function and physical abilities. "There is increasing evidence," Dr. Winter states, "that if you learn a musical instrument in adulthood, take up singing or really concentrate on what an orchestra is playing . . . , these activities will help you: strengthen your body, organize your thinking, and improve your coordination."

11

Concentrate on one sense at a time to sharpen your other senses.

SOMETIMES when I practice the violin, I play in the dark. I close my eyes and listen only to the sounds I'm making. I don't look at my fingers, my bow, or my instrument. I concentrate only on the sound. Then when I open my eyes and play normally again, I'm much more "tuned in" to the pitch and clarity to each note. It enables me to increase my effectiveness at hearing the tonation of my playing. At other times, I study videos of great violinists by shutting off the sound. I concentrate on their movements, on how they draw the bow back and forth and how they move their arms and hands.

Basketball players learn how to shut out the roar of the crowd so they can concentrate on the movement of their bodies and making the free throw. Many lessons in kung fu require that the student shut out all of the senses except for touch, so that he can be guided by the direction of the wind or the texture of the sand upon which he walks.

It doesn't matter which sense you choose. Rotate your focus so that you increase your skill with each sense. Soon they will all come together and all benefit from each other.

If a man wishes to be sure of the road he treads on, he must close his eyes and walk in the dark.

ST. JOHN OF THE CROSS

12

Ask yourself silly questions.

THERE are times when we get so involved in what we're trying to accomplish that we lose all our objectivity. We run out of energy and out of ideas. That's the time to start from a fresh viewpoint. Look at what you're doing from a child's point of view, or from the view of someone totally unfamiliar with your industry or technology. If a child watches you do something and asks the inevitable question, "Why are you doing that?" it makes you stop and think. Is there a good reason for doing something the way you're doing it? Or is it just because "it's always been done that way"?

These are the questions that make us stretch and grow. They're what we need when we are desperately trying to solve a problem and we get blocked and stuck. The silly, crazy questions help us explode out of our limited thought patterns.

In his book, *Brain Workout*, Dr. Arthur Winter suggests that you think of problem solving as playing with blocks. If what you are trying to construct falls apart or doesn't work, just pick up the blocks and try another design. Keep rearranging the blocks until you have created a structure that stands up. Here are some other methods he recommends for getting out of a creative rut:

- *Incubate.* Don't expect all answers to come just when you want them to. Sometimes you have to mull them over for a while until you get a breakthrough.

- *Don't get locked into a role.* If you consider yourself "the practical one" or "the disciplinarian," you're limiting the ways you can approach problems. Let go of old labels.

- *Be disciplined.* Even creativity needs a structured environment—a certain place or time of day when you can work without interruption or distraction.

- *Keep a notebook or tape recorder handy.* You never know when ideas or solutions will make themselves known. If you don't record your thoughts, you often forget them.

- *Don't keep going over the same track.* Following the same path will lead you to the same result. Don't harp on what went wrong; just let it rest and start over again.

- *Defer judgment.* Don't follow ideas with negative thoughts. Give the ideas time to hatch before you decide "That won't work."

- *Don't make excuses.* People of all ages, genders, physical conditions, and economic status have accomplished great things. You can too.

The "silly question" is the first intimation of some totally new development.

ALFRED NORTH WHITEHEAD

13

Search for your untapped reserves.

OVER the years, we absorb millions of bits of knowledge. Large chunks of information, little snippets here and there. We're all huge collectors, whether we're aware of it or not. It might be knowledge we've gotten from reading books, listening to tapes, or watching videos. It might be the lessons learned from hands-on experience. However the knowledge is gained, it remains in our mind's resource library.

However, if that knowledge is not applied, it is lost. We cannot reach our full potential unless we learn to make full use of the resources we have available. And the way we tap into those resources is by taking action. Use it or lose it—it's as simple as that. You can plan and plan and plan forever, but until you take action your knowledge is just taking up valuable brain cells.

Alan Schonberg, founder and chairman of Management Recruiters International, the world's largest search firm, has been in business more than thirty years and has over seven hundred offices nationwide. He believes in the "do it now" theory of action. "If you're going to wait until you're 100 percent prepared," he says, "until you have every *i* dotted and every *t* crossed, you're going to miss a hell of a lot of opportunity. I would much rather take preliminary action, even if I have to tell the other person that I'm only 80 percent prepared. That way I can regroup, come back, be even better prepared than I would have been the first time."

You may be afraid to take action before you're fully prepared. But even if you make three mistakes along the way, you've now gained information, and now have three different ways to improve in the future. When you apply your knowledge to action, it increases the value of what you've learned one hundred times.

Watch inspirational movies.

ONE of my favorite films is *Rudy*. It's about a young boy whose one ambition in life is to play football for Notre Dame University. He's not a great athlete, but that's his dream. And it's only through his tenacity and persistence, despite the odds, that Rudy makes his dream come true.

Watching this movie, you cannot help but be inspired by its message. This young man has to overcome many obstacles and a ton of rejection before he sees his dream come true. But he has the will, the determination, and the hunger. He goes through great moments of despair, but he also gets to experience the thrill of success.

Seeing someone else go through the struggles of life reminds us that we all experience these ups and downs. It also reminds us that passionate action can take us to unbelievable places.

15

Always consider the opposites.

ALL of life is made up of the yin (passive) and the yang (active). No matter how you look at something, there is always another way to view it. You can stare at a puzzle for hours and see no possible solution. Then, suddenly, your viewpoint shifts and the answer becomes blindingly clear. You can be hopelessly lost, turn a corner, and there you are.

Everything is both good and bad, positive and negative. What's good for one person may be bad for another. What's bad at the time (getting fired from your job, for instance) may be a blessing in disguise (opening the door to new opportunities). So in every situation, we should learn to look for, and balance, the yin and yang. When either side is at an extreme, we are in trouble. If we are too passive, nothing will be accomplished. If we are too active, we will burn out before we reach our destination. The aim is always to find the balance between the two.

16

Learn from your successes as well as your failures.

MUCH has been said on the subject of learning from our failures. True failure is not in falling down; it is in failing to get up again, evaluate what went wrong, and start over again.

Sometimes, however, we need to remind ourselves of the lessons we learned from success. When you take a successful action, don't just congratulate yourself and move on. Take a look at that action and see how you may be able to apply it to other areas of your life. There were certain steps you took that led you in a positive direction. Perhaps you can use those steps again, copying them exactly or adapting them to fit a different circumstance.

17

Direct your mind toward nothingness.

I was watching a basketball game one night when B. J. Armstrong, a player for the Hornets, saw his chance to make a basket and win the game for his team. The camera followed him in close-up down the court. There was an expression on his face that told me before he ever made the shot that he would be successful. He was the picture of will and determination. There was no thought behind it. It was pure emotion and energy. He was entirely focused on making that basket. His body was so well trained, he was running on instinct. It's a level of performance where everything is so in sync, the mind and body are working as one, and no conscious thought is involved. That is the level of action we are striving to achieve.

There are five stages of action we can achieve:

1. When we're born, we are unconsciously incompetent. We can't do anything, and we're not even aware of what we cannot do.

2. We move from that stage to being consciously incompetent. We know we are not able to do certain things and that we have to learn how to do them. Young children know they can't do all the things grown-ups can do. They can't wait to get older so that they can learn how to read, write, and play the games that older kids can play.

3. The third phase is being consciously competent. You know what you're doing wrong, and you go about fixing it.

4. The fourth phase is being unconsciously competent—when you've become so competent at a certain skill that it's become a natural part of you. There is no more thought involved. You're so in tune with yourself that you've achieved a "mindless" state, a state of nothingness. This

happens when you put aside all thoughts of displaying your skill or of winning a competition, when you simply become one with the action.

5. The fifth phase is the return to awareness. This phase is essential; with it, you can repeat what you have accomplished in phase four. You can observe and analyze what you have done, and you can do it again. You memorize the feelings you had in the state of nothingness. In sports, for instance, you would memorize your pulse and breathing rates, recall what your feet felt like inside your shoes, how your jersey, soaked with sweat, stuck to the back of your neck. Once you learn to visualize all the different factors, you can bring yourself back to that zone again. You can dive into the waters of peak performance, come out and review your accomplishment, and then dive back into nothingness again.

18

Nature grows to its maximum. Why can't we?

THERE is no excess in nature. A tree grows to its maximum potential, no more, no less. We are living matter, just like a tree. But we have so much more potential. We can move someplace else if we need water, or if we're not getting the nutrients we need. We can build shelter from the rain and wind. We can do all these things, but we get bogged down in our own worries and fears.

Why can't we make our goal in life to be like the tree, and grow to our maximum potential? To do our best in all things, to discover our unique talents, to give back to others in a way that leaves a positive legacy when we go. That's the closest we can come to fulfilling our potential. Why should we settle for anything less?

―――――――――

Men argue, nature acts.

VOLTAIRE

SUMMARY

- Knowledge is the foundation for action. Every action you take provides a lesson for the next.

- You do not need a formal education to be knowledgeable. Much of your education is gained through experience.

- Be objective about your own performance. If all went well, be sure you know what you did right so you can repeat it. If there were glitches, figure out what went wrong and why.

- Realize that the studying and learning you do in one area is transferable to all areas of your life. You're learning how to learn, and by learning that process you can learn everything else in the world.

- Knowledge + belief = confidence. Learn as much as you can about what you're trying to do. Believe in yourself and your abilities. Those two factors combined give you the confidence to push through any obstacles that may arise.

- Solving a problem does not mean you stop searching for knowledge. Often, the answer to one question leads to many other unanswered questions. But it is this cycle of questions and answers that keeps us moving forward in life.

- Life is a balance between yin and yang—the positive and the negative, the active and the passive. There are times when we must be patient and wait for things to come to us; there are other times when we are better off aggressively pursuing our goals. Our aim is to be comfortable within both scenarios, and to find the balance between the two.

· Never settle for anything less than fulfilling your whole potential.

ACTION PLANS

- Tackle problems as if you are a reporter tracking down a story:

  ⇒ Seek out experts.

  ⇒ Ask questions.

  ⇒ Do your own research via books, magazines, newspapers and the Internet.

  ⇒ Come to a conclusion based on other people's advice and suggestions, your research, and your own thoughts and ideas.

- Get objective feedback on your performance. Call at least three people, explain what happened, and ask for their advice.

- Commit at least fifteen minutes each day to learning something new, whether it's factual (reading, listening to audiotapes, researching on the net); artistic (learning to sing, play an instrument, paint, sculpt, craft); skillful (carpentry, computer programs, gardening, cooking, sports); or spiritual (reading, speaking with a spiritual leader, visiting a place of worship).

- Concentrate on one sense at a time. Listen to music with your eyes closed. Watch a sport on TV with the sound off. Focus on the texture of your clothing as you get dressed in the morning. Practice this for a short period every day until you can bring one sense into sharp focus without shutting out the other four senses.

- Ask yourself silly questions. Use your imagination to solve a problem or get yourself out of a rut. Pretend you're an alien from another planet with no knowledge of how things "have always been done" here on earth.

NOTES

ACTION STEPS FOR PLANNING

A S the famous philosopher Yogi Berra once said, "You've got to be careful if you don't know where you're going because you might not get there."

Although Yogi's logic is a bit convoluted, he is on the right track. It's very difficult to get anywhere if you don't know where you're going. It's only when you set goals, make plans, and take actions to carry them out that you can achieve success. Your mind is an amazing mechanism. If you have vague dreams and hopes stuffed away in dark corners of your mind, that's where they will stay. As soon as you expose them to the light of day, as soon as you write them down and keep them visible in front of you, they turn into specific goals that can become reality. Planning is the instrument that teaches your mind to tell your body what to do.

If you want to take smarter, more efficient actions, you've got to plan them. It's a directional signal that keeps you focused and on track. Every single day we have a new opportunity to build our future. Planning helps us get from day one to day two to the rest of our lives.

19

Pare down to the bare essentials.

ONE of the problems of being constantly bombarded with new opportunities is that I tend to go off on tangents. This can be a good thing, because tangents can lead you to the most interesting places. But, as in everything in life, there must be a balance. It is all too easy to go off on a tangent and lose your way back. Although it's entirely possible to juggle many aspects of life at once (all of us do), we can sometimes get overwhelmed and confused by demands pulling us in many directions at once.

When you find yourself off on a tangent, stop and ask yourself a few questions before you get too far off track. There was probably a reason you got off on a tangent in the first place. Can you remember what that reason was? Write it down so you don't forget it when you want to come back to it. Is the tangent leading toward your goal, or away from it? Some tangents can lead you through a side door and take you right to your destination. Some, however, can lead you to a maze that is difficult to escape.

The best way to keep yourself from going off on tangents is through planning. That is not to say you can never take spontaneous action. There are times when immediate decisions are called for, and they must be made. "Immediate," however, is a relative term. We often put unnecessary pressure on ourselves to make hasty decisions. If someone presents us with an idea or opportunity, we can feel obligated to say "yes" or "no" on the spot.

There is nothing wrong with saying, "That's a great idea. Let me think about it and I'll get back to you tomorrow." This is a lesson I've been learning lately. People present ideas to me all the time, and I have a tendency to get excited about them and say, "All right! Let's do that!" Now I've learned to say, "Let me think about it for a day or so." The next day I bounce the ideas off three other people and hear what they have to say about it. I kick the idea around and often come up with an even better one. Sometimes I realize that it's not a good idea after all, and giving it extra thought saves me from committing to something that would have been a waste of time. Either way, I'm taking qualified action.

In my book *Diamonds Under Pressure*, I developed the acronym FOCUS as a tool to help regain control in your life and take the actions you need to move forward. FOCUS has five facets:

- *Foresight and Faith:* Before you can take any effective action, you must have a clear idea of where you want to go, and you must believe that you are going to get there. This combination of foresight and faith is what inspires us to put in the effort necessary to make our dreams possible.

- *Organization:* The most successful people know that nothing is ever achieved in one giant leap. It's the tiny steps you take, one by one, that help you reach your destination. The most successful people also believe in the importance of setting goals, both short- and long-term. In order to transform your dreams and visions into reality, you must begin by putting your goals down in writing and breaking them down into small, tangible steps that can be achieved one at a time. Once you begin to make practical, reality-based plans for your future, that future can become a reality.

- *Concentrated Effort and Courage:* Once you have a clear vision of where you want to go, a belief that you can get there, and step-by-step goals to guide you toward your objective, the real work begins. When we watch an athlete like Bruce Jenner break a world's record, we see his moment of triumph. We don't see all the years of training that went into that moment. There is a basic truth behind the old cliché "No pain, no gain." The rewards you get out of any endeavor depend on the amount of effort you put into it. Most people who don't achieve as much as they want to in life don't fall short because of lack of ability, but because they gave up too soon. Those who do achieve know that it is only concentrated, focused effort that will produce results.

  Along with concentrated effort, the C in FOCUS stands for courage. Nothing of importance is gained without risk. Courage does not mean ignoring our day-to-day realities, nor does it mean taking foolhardy risks that might endanger ourselves or our families. Courage does mean taking carefully evaluated risks, facing the fears that may be holding us back, and taking appropriate actions to move toward our goals.

- *Understanding:* There are two aspects to understanding. The first has to do with comprehending why it is we don't do the things we dream of doing. One of the main reasons is fear. Fear is a powerful emotion that can stop us from achieving many things of which we are capable, and convince us that our dreams of achievement and success are simply impossible.

   Everyone experiences fear. That is a good thing because it makes us stop and think, and often keeps us from making foolish choices. However, if we let fear run our lives, we can spend many precious hours imagining dire consequences that will never come to pass. So it's important to understand and acknowledge our fears, but not to let fear stop us from taking thoughtful action.

   We come to that thoughtful action through the second aspect of understanding, which has to do with gathering all the information you can about the subject in which you are interested. There are thousands of resources available to us today, from bookstores and libraries to the Internet and those people who have gone before us, most of whom are more than willing to share their insights and experiences. What you want to do is collect as much information as possible so that you can make intelligent decisions about taking action. Every time you get a new piece of information, you move closer to your destination. Understanding builds confidence and strengthens faith. It also tells you where you need to concentrate your efforts and what actions you need to take next to achieve your goal.

- *Seeding and Service:* A certain phenomenon occurs when you reach out to other people for help and guidance. You are planting seeds for your future. Every person with whom you speak is a potential connection. Not every person will be able to help you reach your goal, but you never know. And you never know whom that person knows, or might meet in the future. You have to be planting your seeds all the time, because you never know which ones will bear the most fruit.

The *S* in FOCUS also stands for service, which means giving back to others. When you ask high achievers to define success, you'll hear all kinds of answers, usually involving pride in their performance, in their families, in having achieved certain goals. They never mention money, fame, or worldly goods. They talk about personal values, inner resources, and doing something worthwhile with their lives. No one will deny that money is important, but it usually comes as a by-product of other achievements.

The true key to living a successful life lies in taking actions that not only benefit oneself, but benefit others as well. Whenever you find yourself off track, recognize that your center of focus is turned inward, toward yourself. As soon as you turn yourself around, everything will come back to you tenfold when you focus on helping others. The more you can affect other people's lives for the better, the greater your success becomes.

When you keep these five steps in mind, every action you take will be specific, directed, and designed to move you closer to success. The reason that the FOCUS acronym is so powerful is that it takes the difficulties in life and pares them down to their bare essentials—which, it turns out, is the only real way to get anything done. The loftiest goals and most complicated tasks must be broken down into tiny, simple steps that, taken together, enable you to travel long distances. Every action you take should be broken down to its simplest components so that you are not moving around in chaos, but are taking qualified, specific actions in the right direction. As Bernard Baruch once said, "Whatever failures I have known, whatever errors I have committed, whatever follies I have witnessed in private and public life have been the consequence of action without thought."

Planning is like a road map. It can show us the right way, keep us going in the right direction when we're not sure which way to turn. It means recognizing where we are now, and finding the best ways to get to where we want to be. Planning is a bridge we build from our dreams to our goals.

20

The best tools are often the simplest.

COMPUTERIZED appointment calendars and time management programs are great tools. But in my opinion they will never take the place of a simple, hand-written to-do list. There's something about writing things down, putting the pen to the paper, that glues them to your memory bank. We often have a misplaced trust in our computers' memories; it's only when we suffer a technological breakdown that we realize in some ways we were much better off with a pad and pencil.

I have nothing against computers. It's just that they are not always the answer for every ill. Roger Dow, vice president and general sales manager of Marriott Lodging, tells this story about how simplicity can win over computers. About ten years ago, Dow received a comment from a loyal Marriott customer. Her complaint was that although she was a frequent customer at the same hotel, every time she came into a Marriott she was treated like a stranger. Dow agreed that something should be done, and went to see the people in the technology department. He wanted to know if they could devise a computer program that would recognize repeat customers. Sure, they said, they could do it. Of course, it would cost about four million dollars and take three or four years to develop (keep in mind that this was ten years ago). Management decided such a system would not be cost-effective.

A few weeks later, Dow himself traveled to a Marriott in Irvine, California. He was greeted by a doorman named Bill, whom Dow had known for many years. Bill took Dow's bags and then introduced him to the woman behind the counter, someone Dow had never seen before.

"How do you do, Mr. Dow," she said. "Welcome back to the Marriott, we're so glad to see you again."

Dow asked if they had ever met before. "No, we haven't," she said. "I've only been here three weeks."

"Then how do you know I've been here before?" asked Dow.

The woman explained that when a customer came into the hotel, he was greeted by Bill. If Bill didn't know the customer, he would say, "What's your name?" and ask, "Have you stayed with us before?" If the customer said yes, Bill would pull on his earlobe when he introduced the customer to the person working the desk.

"Watch this," said the woman. She called over a bellman. "This is Mr. Dow and he's staying with us on the concierge level this evening," she said, and pulled her earlobe.

"Good evening, Mr. Dow," said the bellman. "It's so nice to have you staying with us again."

Dow was very impressed with their system. "All of a sudden it hit me," he says. "Here I was looking at a multimillion-dollar computer system, when something as simple as pulling an earlobe really works. Computer systems are great, but 90 percent of the time it's all about ear pulls!"

I couldn't agree more. For me, simpler is better. A few nights ago I was looking at my desk, trying to organize myself for the next day's work. Because I work on several different projects at once, I had four different pads in front of me. Each contained a to-do list for one particular area. Looking at the four lists, I realized it was time to reevaluate my system. Having four separate lists was not working for me. So I combined them into one list of things to do and people to call. That way I knew I could sit down at my desk in the morning, see at one glance exactly what I needed to do, and get started right away.

21

Take a lesson from the spider.

THERE is one simple tool I use to keep myself organized. I call it my spiderweb. I am a great believer in visual reminders of all sorts. My office is totally decorated with reminders of past accomplishments as well as visual representations of my goals and dreams.

One of those representations is what I call the spiderweb, which I draw on a big white board hanging on the wall beside my desk. At the center of the web is my business. Many strands emanate from that center circle, each one labeled and representing a different area of my business. Like a spiderweb, each individual strand has other strands attached to it. These strands are also labeled with the names of people involved with these projects, or with steps that have to be taken to complete the project.

Spiders are nature's brilliant engineers. Their webs are incredibly strong, yet almost invisible. Spiders eat insects that become trapped in their web. Once the spider has eaten its meal, it returns to the center of the web to determine whether or not the strands have been damaged. If the web has been torn in several places from heavy activity, it reconstructs the whole thing. If the catch was low and the web is not heavily damaged, it will be reused after minor repairs are made.

Every morning, I start off my day by focusing on the center of the web. Like a spider, I survey my web and see where it is standing strong and where it needs work. I check my to-do list against my web and make sure that all my strands are getting the attention they deserve and that there are no gaping holes. I might have some new strands to add, or I might erase some that no longer apply.

This allows me to get a glimpse at the "big picture" before I take on the individual tasks of the day. Looking at the web, I may get ideas on how different strands might connect with each other. And it enables me to determine if the actions I'm planning to take that day are targeted in the right areas and to figure out what percentage of time I need to spend on each strand.

The spiderweb can be used to keep track of multiple projects, or to divide one project into smaller segments. For instance, as I write this book, I keep the theme of "taking action" as the spider in the center and each category of action as a strand coming off that center circle. Each category then has strands representing the various topics I want to cover in those pages. If you're a salesperson, each strand could represent a different prospect or client, with the smaller strands as reminders of the steps you need to take to either close or service that customer. If you're a musician, each strand could represent a different piece of music that must be learned and practiced before a concert. No matter what your occupation, the spiderweb can be a useful tool to help your planning and organization.

22

Prioritize everything.

WHEN the drudgery of the day-to-day tasks you're performing sets in, one tool you can use to get through it is prioritizing. Sometimes drudgery sets in when you're off track, when you're doing too many things at once and not focusing on the ones that are most important. When that happens, it's time to put things in order.

This process accomplishes several things. It gives you a chance to reorganize yourself. Perhaps there is a step you've forgotten. Maybe you're doing something that isn't entirely necessary. Maybe your original goal has shifted slightly, but you haven't shifted your priorities along with it. You might come up with a more creative approach than the one you've been using. When you do this kind of prioritization, it clears your mind and lets you know (a) that you are on the right track or (b) that you need to be moving in a different direction.

Prioritizing and renewing your focus also refuels your energy levels. It's like an architect designing and redesigning the plans for a house. It's very exciting when the drawings are complete. But as the job goes on and the building is actually constructed, adjustments must be made. Reality presents certain problems that cannot be anticipated on paper. The architect keeps the blueprint in sight at all times to remind him of his original intentions, but makes necessary changes as he goes along.

I do the same by keeping my spiderweb on the wall next to my desk, by keeping my to-do lists up to date, and by writing down my long- and short-term goals. I check them every day to remind myself of my original intentions. In the course of daily business, I make changes and adjustments. But the reminders I see around me keep me focused and get me back on track when I suddenly realize I'm spending time doing paperwork that doesn't really need to be done for three months, or getting off on a tangent that takes me away from my true destination.

Sometimes, one project or one aspect of your life becomes so time-consuming that you neglect other areas. It may be necessary to put all your focus on this one area for a time in order to accomplish certain goals. But then there comes the time when you need to get your life back on an even keel again. This happened to me recently when I spent a large portion of my time selling and marketing a book for an important client. When the intensity of this project began to wane, I knew I had to get my core business back on course again.

I went down to my office and cleared my desk of everything but a single sheet of paper. I wrote down everything I could think of that would bring income back to my business, everyone I could call, fax, or e-mail. I went through my files and my old to-do lists to see whom I could call. I put these names in order on the left-hand side of the page, and on the right I listed what actions I needed to take. The next morning, I knew exactly what I needed to do to revitalize my income-producing activities.

This kind of prioritization and revitalization has two benefits. First, it allows you to refocus on those tasks that are most important to you, that will lead you most directly toward your goal. And second, it's an energy builder. When your priorities are jumbled, when you're not sure what the next steps should be, you lose your clarity and vision. But when you bring that goal back into focus again, it pumps you up. Your adrenaline starts flowing and you're ready to get back to work.

23

For each project you consider, evaluate how much time you can afford to spend on it.

ESTABLISH the value of the project. Will it increase your income? Prestige? Move your career forward? Bring you closer to your goals? Write down the potential benefits for you and for others it may involve or affect.

Now write down all the negatives involved. How difficult is this job going to be? Are you working with other people? If so, will they be accessible to you when you need them? Will this job take an unreasonable (or unmanageable) amount of time away from other projects or from your friends and family?

You now have three options. You can pass on the project. You can say yes to the project, on a limited basis (perhaps as a silent partner or consultant). Or you can make a commitment to giving your best effort to it.

Check your dollars and cents for motivation.

WHETHER you're going through good times or bad, it's very easy to let your true financial picture slip into the background. Sometimes when I need a motivator to keep me pumped up and action-oriented, I take out one piece of paper and write down all my outgoing expenses. Seeing that number can be an instant energizer. It also allows me to see where I might be able to cut back, to spend less in certain areas. It helps me to see how I can begin to save money, perhaps even put it toward a particular goal. I make a list of investment priorities, and it helps me to see how much I will need for each goal, how much I currently have to work with, and how I can reallocate funds to make future goals possible.

Then I write down all my incoming moneys. When I do this exercise, it focuses me on where my money is coming from. My business has several different income-producing segments. When I go through my records I can see exactly which segments of my business are bringing in the most money. That lets me know where I should be devoting my time and attention. It allows me to focus on what activities I should spend time on to produce more income. If you're on a steady salary, you might use this review to figure out how you can get a better bonus, or a promotion to the next income level.

This is my financial checkup. Just as I have periodic physical checkups to be sure that I am healthy, I need to conduct periodic financial checkups to make sure my money situation is in good shape.

25

Keep your vision clear, your goal out in front, and never forget the fundamentals.

Don Storms, one of the most successful multilevel marketers in the country, was talking about things in his life that he regrets. He didn't have many, but one that stood out was something he said to his son. When his son was in school, a teacher explained that his son spent too much time dreaming in class. Don reprimanded the child and told him he must do his classwork and not be dreaming.

Storms, who now believes that having a dream is one of the most important things you can do in life, can't believe he ever said such a thing. He now tells everyone he knows (including his son) that there are three things that pull you forward in life:

- *A clear vision:* A vision is what a dream turns into. Dreams can be vague and indefinite, but a vision is clear, specific, and well-defined.

- *A goal:* The goal is what pulls you forward and helps you outline the individual steps you must take to make your vision a reality.

- *The fundamentals:* These are the basic activities you must keep performing in order to remain on course. Fundamentals include the tedious, day-to-day tasks that must be completed as well as the standards and ethics upon which your life and business are built.

Create a mission statement.

A mission statement should reflect your sense of purpose and guide all your actions. It should be simple, focused, and practical. Roger Dow of Marriott Lodging thought his company's mission statement was too long and complicated. So he simplified it to state: "Every customer leaves satisfied." There is no ambiguity there, nothing anyone could misunderstand. It says it all.

I have a mission statement for my company too. It reads: "To serve the worldwide community providing individuals and organizations with practical tools and information that will significantly increase their value and performance in the area of sales, management and personal development. To carry out this mission, we constantly strive to practice what we preach."

I have this mission statement printed on a whiteboard hanging on my wall next to my desk. All I have to do is turn my head to remind myself of why I do what I do. This is what keeps me going, and keeps me on track.

Those who cannot tell what they desire or expect still sigh and struggle with indefinite thoughts and vast wishes.

RALPH WALDO EMERSON

27

Rehearse every action in your mind before you take it.

VISUALIZATION is an "inside secret" all successful people know about and practice. It's really mental rehearsal of positive scenarios. If you can actually see yourself standing up at the podium receiving the "most together person" award, the greater your chances of getting it. Great athletes visualize winning performances all the time. Great musicians practice all the time, whether or not they have their instruments with them. They can see, hear, and feel the instrument almost as if they were actually playing it.

You can rehearse every action in your mind before you take it. Before you make a phone call or go into a meeting, visualize a successful outcome (don't try to construct a scenario of exactly what's going to happen step by step—you can't expect other people involved to respond exactly the way you picture them). When you're about to start a new project, see it finished—and finished well—in your mind's eye.

Seeing things in his mind's eye is one of the special talents of America's preeminent mentalist, the Amazing Kreskin. He once challenged two champion chess players that he could play them both simultaneously—blindfolded. He had a month to practice. Kreskin is not a chess player; at that time, he'd only played about ten games in his entire life. So every day for that month, he went hiking in the mountains for five or six hours. "I did nothing but picture moves," he says. "The queen to this position, the pawn straight ahead. Of course I didn't win, but it took them two hours to beat me. I simply did what every chess player does—think ahead to the next best move."

Kreskin has his own thoughts about visualization. "The word 'visualization' doesn't simply mean using the sense of vision," he says. People have many senses, and some are stronger than others. Imagine that several people go to a restaurant to share a meal. They all agree that it was a great place. If you were to ask what they each liked about it, you might end up with a variety of answers. One person might say, "I loved the wallpaper and the colors of decor." Another might say, "I loved the accents the waiters had, and the music that was playing in the background." Another might say, "I enjoyed it so much. The tablecloth was so smooth and soft, the chairs were upholstered in velvet, and the floors were cold marble I could feel through my shoes." So if someone says to you, "Picture this," and you are having difficulty seeing it, try thinking of the sounds you might hear or the textures you might encounter. "It's all visualization," says Kreskin. "You just adapt it to your own strongest sense."

28

Learn to trust yourself.

FOR many people, this is one of the most difficult lessons in life. We spend a lot of time looking to others to tell us how we're supposed to behave or what we're supposed to be feeling. We want their approval and affection. There are certain situations, however, in which we have to rely on our own strengths and abilities to get us through.

Soprano Judith Von Houser has discovered this from being onstage. Von Houser has performed with the New York Grand Opera, the Des Moines Metro Opera, and many other companies. An opera singer has an enormous amount of material to remember. At first, she was afraid that she would forget her part during a performance. Then she learned to trust.

"You might forget for five seconds," she says, "but then it will come back to you. You have to learn to trust yourself, to relax and breathe and trust that it will come back. You let it flow. If you've done your work and preparation beforehand, it will be there when you need it. It's when you try to stop the flow and think about it that you get into trouble."

The key, of course, is the preparation. It's like the old cliché about riding a bicycle. It takes a while to learn how to ride. After many attempts, you suddenly find that you have mastered the skills it takes to balance and propel yourself forward. The next time you get on the bike, you don't have to learn these skills over again. But you do have to trust that they have stayed with you. You may be wobbly for the first few minutes if you haven't ridden in a long time, but soon enough you are steady and strong again. If you try to think about the mechanics of riding the bike, you'll be tipped over and on the ground before you know it.

The same principles apply in any situation. Once you've done the work and have mastered the skills, it's all a matter of trust.

29

Detach yourself.

THIS is a paradox. The story of the Zen student and the master who almost drowned him tells us that we must be so hungry for what we want that it is as important to us as our next breath. That is true. However, it is also true that we cannot be so obsessed with our desires that we are overcome by them.

When you are so attached to your desires, you sometimes become blinded by them. Your thinking becomes cloudy and unfocused. Insecurity makes you believe that if you don't own that car, achieve the presidency, meet the right mate, make a certain amount of money, live a particular lifestyle, or reach a specific goal, you will not be able to go on with your life. Everything is riding on that one desire.

There is nothing wrong with desire itself. Your goals must be of value to you. There must be something at stake in order to keep you motivated. However, you can't let your whole life be determined by the success or failure to achieve this one desire. Step back and look at your goals objectively. Better opportunities may arise along the way: If you are blinded by obsession, you may miss these opportunities altogether.

There is another drawback to obsessive desire. It makes you selfish. It clouds your vision about how your actions may be affecting others—your family, friends, neighbors, and coworkers. You can't think of anything but *your* goals, *your* desires. It allows you to justify harming others to achieve your goals. When you want something that badly, it stops you from giving back to others. There is no pride, satisfaction, or happiness to be gained from achieving an unworthy goal.

The true value of a human being can be found in the degree to which he has attained liberation from the self.

ALBERT EINSTEIN

30

Change direction.

YOU never know how things will turn out until you begin taking action. No matter how carefully and thoroughly you plan, you can never be sure you're going in the right direction until you start moving. There is an old saying: The map is not the territory. You can plan your route by studying the map, but until you explore the territory, there can be no true understanding of what actually lies ahead.

When you start on the journey toward your goal, your plan tells you to move in certain directions. But when you actually start moving, you may find there are better routes to take. Don't get stuck on one road just because it's on the map. New facts may appear, unexpected situations may present themselves. That's when it's time to reevaluate, to make a new map, to change directions. Most of the time, you will find that the new direction leads you on a straighter path to your goal.

31

Plan your creative attack.

WHAT you're striving for is speed and depth. Every action should be performed efficiently—which means that you can't skip steps just to get something done quickly. Speed is important, but not if it means sacrificing quality. So when you're planning an "attack" for reaching a goal, you must think creatively. What is the best route to move from A to B? Sometimes the straightest route is the best; sometimes you get more out of taking the scenic route.

Most people don't reach their goals because they give up too soon. They run into obstacles or barriers, experience failures, and stop trying. They think they've done everything they can and have run out of options. They feel stuck. This feeling is seldom based in reality, however. There are many ways to get yourself "unstuck," to start thinking on a new level, to pump up the energy and get over the hurdles.

Here are some ways to get yourself moving when you're feeling stuck:

- *Throw the situation out to people you trust.* Explain the steps you've taken and the obstacles you've run into. Ask them what they would do next. It's often easier for an outsider to be objective and see things we might have missed.

- *Make a "massive action" list.* Tell yourself there are twenty steps you can take to move forward, and start writing them down. Don't censor yourself, even if the steps seem ridiculous or impossible. They may just lead you to a practical idea you can use.

- *Concentrate on the details.* Sometimes we get stuck because we're trying to accomplish everything at once. We're looking at the final goal and not taking the small steps we must take to get there. So make the calls you've been putting off, send out thank-you notes, do some research on the Internet. You just might come up with the one piece of information you're missing in order to move ahead.

32

Remain close to your heart.

WHEN you take on a project, you make a commitment to it. If that commitment is missing, you're more likely to quit before you get to the finish line. The more there is at stake, the greater your commitment must be.

Taking action is a combination of movement and attitude. Each one is less effective alone than both are taken together. In extreme situations, the will to succeed is very important, but so is taking the action that moves you forward. This was demonstrated in the movie *Apollo 13*. Three astronauts are stranded in space, and the ground crew in Houston must figure out how to bring them home. People are coming up with ideas, but most of the thinking is leading to what cannot be done. Finally, the head of the crew turns to his men and says, "Failure is not an option." It is a turning point in their thinking. They forget about what is "impossible" and begin to think in terms of what they can accomplish with what is available to them. And they did, of course, accomplish their mission—they brought the astronauts home alive.

With so much at stake, with no room for error, our actions take on an energy all their own. But these crisis situations are not everyday occurrences. Most of the time, we're facing much more mundane problems—and we must find some way in ourselves to infuse our actions with our own energy. We must constantly tell ourselves that failure is not an option. We must have what Brian Tracy, best-selling author of *The Luck Factor*, calls a "go-forward philosophy." That means having a vision of the future and moving toward it.

"I always resolve to make the next twelve months the best twelve months of my life," says Tracy. "No matter what has happened, I look forward to the next twelve months to make them better." The way to do that is to project yourself forward to the next year (or three years or five years). You look ahead to where you want to be, and then ask yourself, "What do I have to do today to get where I want to go?"

What would your life look like if it was perfect five years from now? How much money would you be making? Where would you be living? How healthy would you be? How would you describe your lifestyle? Write all these things down. Most people do not even know the answers to these questions. Those who do answer these questions, those who take the time to develop these pictures and write them down, have a 100 percent better chance of achieving their goals.

This visualization not only helps you focus on what you want to do—it also helps you weed out those things that are taking you away from your main goals. You can't do everything at once. There are times when you may have to sacrifice some things (even if it's just temporarily) so that the projects closest to your heart can thrive.

It is only with the heart that one can see rightly; what is essential is invisible to the eye.

ANTOINE DE SAINT-EXUPÉRY

33

Act as if success is already yours.

WALK it, think it, speak it, be it. Put reminders up on your walls. Write your goals down and look at them frequently. Build your spiderweb around them. Make your success as tangible as possible long before it actually happens.

Your mind is the best place to build success. My cousin Peter Kofitsas is a very passionate and motivated student who spent several years working and studying so that he could attend New York Medical College. He finally achieved his goal. On his first day on campus he could barely take it all in. But suddenly, sitting on a bench enjoying his surroundings, he had a vision. He saw himself an established physical therapist, head of a cutting-edge wellness center. He was on a television talk show, along with his wife, talking about his plans for the future. That vision was so clear and strong, he now uses it for inspiration and motivation. This is not a wish or dream for him. It is the future he knows will be his, and all his actions are geared in its direction.

The key to acting as if success is already yours is to write down your goals in the present tense. If you have a financial goal, don't write: "I will make $75,000 by the year 2001." Write: "I make $75,000 a year." If your goal is to write the great American novel, don't set your goal by saying, "I will finish my novel within two years." Instead, say, "My novel is being published and becoming a bestseller."

A few years ago I had new business cards printed up. They were printed with my two company names, Farber Training Systems and the Diamond Group. Beneath the company names I listed the businesses I was involved in: seminars/radio/TV/literary agency. This was before I even had a television show and before I had any clients in my literary agency. But these were more than just goals to me, they were reality. I didn't wait for each business to be thriving before I put it on the card. Now each business is growing steadily, and each category has been accomplished.

34

Seeing is believing.

I keep my surroundings full of reminders of where I've been and where I want to go. There are times, especially during rough periods, when we all need visual cues to keep our goals in mind. I often talk about the amazing power of visualization, and how we become what we think about. But Marriott's Roger Dow has one caveat about setting goals and visualizing our futures. He warns against setting our boundaries too close and selling ourselves short. Don't box yourself in by telling yourself, "I can never do that," or "I'm just what I am now and I'll never be anything else."

"You have to be careful about how you define yourself," says Dow. "Everyone has the ability to look beyond where they are right now. You never know where life is going to take you. Don't set your parameters too tight. Every single successful person I know tells me that in a million years they never would have dreamed they would be where they are today. But part of the reason they got there was that they allowed themselves to dream big dreams."

Dow also has a system for setting goals to help make those big dreams a reality. Imagine yourself five years from now. You are at an awards banquet, and you are receiving the "most together person in the world" award for doing exactly what you want to be doing. You're walking up to accept your award when one of the organizers grabs your arm and whispers in your ear, "When you receive your award, we'd really like you to describe what it is you do during a typical working day."

As you walk on, another organizer catches your arm. "What the audience really wants to know," he says, "is how you got started. What was the first thing you had to do to get started toward your goal five years ago?"

Organizer number three taps you on the shoulder before you can take another step. "You know," she says, "people love to hear about hard times and obstacles. Please talk about the three biggest obstacles you had to overcome to get to this day."

Finally, just as you're about to step up to the podium, the last organizer catches your attention and says, "Don't forget the thank-you's. Tell us about friends, family members, and mentors who helped you along the way."

"Write out the speech you would make at this awards banquet and *voila!* You've now got a five-year plan to reach your goal," says Dow. "You know where you want to go. You know the first step you have to take to get there. You've come to grips with a few obstacles you are likely to face, and you've identified some people who can help you through the process. You've painted a visual picture, and now you can start moving in that direction."

These, then, are my last words to you: Be not afraid of life. Believe that life is worth living and your belief will help create the fact.

WILLIAM JAMES

35

Keep your goals in plain view.

YOUR physical surroundings can be a great source of energy and inspiration. Over the years many people have proclaimed, "You are what you think about." You can't help but think about what surrounds you. If your surroundings are dark, dreary, and depressing, they will dampen your energy and produce dark, dreary, and depressing thoughts. If, however, you surround yourself with positive, uplifting images, you will benefit from their energizing effects and affirmative influences.

What do your surroundings look like? Is your home filled with things that make you feel good? And what about your work space? Most of us spend many waking hours at work. What does your office look like? Does it represent just another day's drudgery to you? Or does it have reminders of your goals in full view? Do you have anything there that can stimulate energy production? Even the smallest cubicle has room for some personal touches. Perhaps you have a favorite photo or an inspirational quote you can hang on the wall in front of you. Even something as simple as a three-by-five-inch index card with the word "today" on it can be a great motivator.

One of my clients tells me that he keeps his main goals on a sheet of paper wrapped around his wallet. That way, every time he pays for something, he is reminded of his goals. Every time he spends money, he's reminded of how he makes money. His goals are constantly in view. He doesn't have to stop and read the paper every time he takes out the wallet; just knowing that they're there triggers his mind and brings his goals into focus.

You can also surround yourself with reminders of things you have achieved in the past, actions you took that brought about positive results, things you hope to achieve in the future, and the actions you need to take to make those things happen. And, if you work at home, as so many people do these days, you have an even greater opportunity to design your surroundings so that they inspire you to greater heights.

Be selective about what you keep in view. Keep only those things that remind you of goals, activities, and events that show progress, that make you feel good about yourself. These reminders will keep you focused and on track.

See yourself as successful every day.

MANY people have narrow guidelines for their own success. They say, "When I accomplish this, I will be successful." "When I get to this income level, I will be successful." "When I get my dream house, then I will be successful." Success for them can only happen when something very specific is obtained or achieved. But you can't always look for success in the future. If you spend all your time doing that, you will forget about today.

The Amazing Kreskin has some advice on that subject. He believes that at the end of each day, you should find something beneficial that came out of the day, some source of satisfaction that made your day a success. It could be that you passed someone worse off than you on the street and you gave them a helping hand, or smiled at them and got a smile in return. That's when you've achieved success.

"You can't be so rigid about setting your goals for success," he says. "You've got to be flexible. Be like a pilot who has a destination in mind. If the weather becomes bad or challenging, he finds another route. He may have to go out of his way. He may have to lay over for a few hours. But he will get there eventually.

"In the long run, success is not money, it's not your material possessions. There are times when you may be better off relishing a quieter, simpler way of life. Success is not achieved by lying in a plush chair or wearing a velvet jacket. The bottom line is, can you be with your friends and family and have personal comfort and satisfaction. If the answer is yes, then you are successful."

Ten minutes before you go to sleep, plan for tomorrow's success.

SLEEP is an amazing phenomenon. While we are asleep, part of our brain is resting and building up energy for the next day's activities. But another part is working through the many things that are on our minds. That's what dreams are all about. That's also why it often happens that you go to sleep thinking about a problem you just can't seem to solve and wake up in the morning with the solution right in front of you.

Our minds are very open to information during the period just before we go to sleep. This presleep period, often called the hypnoidal period, is a very sensitive time. When parents tell young children not to watch horror movies before they go to bed, they are giving good advice. There's a good chance those images will stay in the child's mind during the night and produce truly frightening nightmares.

You can also put that hypnoidal period to good use. The Amazing Kreskin says that this is a good time to give your brain a problem to solve. Find three or four key words that capsulize your problem. For instance, suppose you have a meeting Thursday night with Alexis, and you have to come up with a creative presentation. Write down the words *Alexis, meeting,* and *Thursday.* Say them to yourself a few times as you fall asleep. Then just leave them. As you're sleeping, your mind will be working on the problem.

The trick is to be able to capture the solution when you wake up. Sometimes we lose the answers because we can't remember them in the morning. Kreskin advises keeping a tape recorder or pad and pencil next to your bed so that you can record your ideas as soon as you wake up.

38

To understand who you are is to understand who you were.

APPRECIATE your own growth and movement. Look back at who you were five or ten years ago. How did you think then? What actions did you take then? How are your thoughts different now? How are your actions different now? Think of how much you have learned in the time that has passed.

All that has gone before was practice for all that is still to come. All the actions you took in the past are the foundation for you to act upon today. You build upon your successes as well as your failures. It is exciting and inspiring to know that every action I perform today has a direct effect on how my life will turn out tomorrow.

39

Become the archer, the arrow, and the target.

IN *Zen in the Art of Archery*, Eugen Herrigel says that "fundamentally, the marksman aims at himself." You are what you are aiming at. You become what you think about. You are both the dream and the dreamer.

You are the archer. You're the one with the power to shoot your arrow in any direction. No one else can do this for you. Someone may teach you how to use the bow, maybe even help you pull it back the first few times you shoot. After that, it is up to you.

You are the arrow. You are the force that is heading in the direction of your goal. Winds may push you from side to side, and you may fall short of the target, but you always have the opportunity to fly forward again.

You are the target. The target is where you've visualized yourself to be once you reach your goal; the bull's-eye is the person you've become along the way.

Once you become the bull's-eye (the vision of where you want to go), the arrow (you) has a clear and logical path to its final destination.

40

Set realistic goals—then add one that makes everyone laugh.

IT'S important to set realistic goals. You can't jump off the roof of a ten-story building with the goal of landing unharmed on the street below. That is a truly impossible goal.

However, at least one of your goals should be something that would make other people laugh and say, "You! You could never do that!" If it's something that your heart truly desires, write it down. You never know where life is going to lead you or what you can accomplish. Most of the time, when we look back at the goals we set for ourselves years ago, we're amazed at how we set them so low, or that we thought we "couldn't do it." That's because we don't know our own potential. Often the goal that seemed so funny to everyone else is the one that gives you the last laugh.

SUMMARY

- Remember the FOCUS acronym:

    ⇒ **F**oresight and Faith
    ⇒ **O**rganization
    ⇒ **C**oncentrated Effort and Courage
    ⇒ **U**nderstanding
    ⇒ **S**eeding and Service

- Planning is the bridge we build from our dreams to our goals. The only real way to get things done is to break goals down into their simplest components and accomplish one task at a time.

- If a project becomes overwhelming or seems to be stuck in place, stop, prioritize and renew your focus toward your original goal. This will refuel your energy level and allow you to concentrate on the steps you need to take next without worrying about all the other things you "should" be doing.

- There are three factors that pull you forward in life:

    ⇒ A clear vision that is specific and well-defined
    ⇒ A goal that helps you determine the steps you must take to make your vision a reality
    ⇒ Remembering the fundamentals, the basic, day-to-day tasks that must be performed in order to remain on course

- Visualization is a mental rehearsal of positive scenarios. It is a secret all successful people share. Rehearse every new action in your mind before you take it, and visualize a successful outcome.

- No matter how carefully and thoroughly you plan, you can never be sure you're going in the right direction until you start moving. Don't get so stuck on the plan you have made that you can't respond to better opportunities that may come along.

- Keep your goals in plain view. You can't help but think about what surrounds you. Surround yourself with reminders of things you have achieved in the past, actions you took that brought about positive results. Choose only those things that make you feel good about yourself.

ACTION PLANS

- Start off each day by making a simple to-do list, then cross off each task as it is accomplished.

- Create a visual reminder system for yourself, such as the spiderweb. Place it somewhere you can view it daily. Use it to remind yourself of the big picture you are trying to construct, as well as the individual tasks that must be tended to.

- Evaluate each new opportunity before you jump into it:

  ⇒ Write down all potential benefits for you and for others it may affect.
  ⇒ List any negatives involved—including how much time and effort it will take, and how it will affect projects you're already involved in.
  ⇒ Weigh the two lists and choose one of these options:

    ⇒ Pass on the project.
    ⇒ Say yes, but on a limited basis.
    ⇒ Commit yourself to it 100 percent.

- Conduct a financial checkup to make sure you're in healthy fiscal condition—and to get yourself motivated:

  ⇒ List your outgoing expenses.
  ⇒ List all sources of income.
  ⇒ Balance one list against the other to help make decisions about revising your budgeting and investment priorities.

- Create a mission statement that defines your goals, reflects your sense of purpose, and guides all your actions.

- Write out five goals you would like to accomplish within the next twelve months. Be specific, and use the present tense. Don't say, "I'm going to be making twice as much as I do now." Write: "I make $100,000." Don't say, "I'm going to become more athletic." Write: "I go to the gym three times a week."

- Practice Brian Tracy's "go-forward philosophy." Project yourself forward in time, and picture yourself as you want to be. Describe your life in detail and *write it all down* (people who write down their goals have a 100 percent better chance of achieving them). Then ask yourself, "What do I have to do today to get where I want to go?"

- Keep a pad and pencil or tape recorder next to your bed. Just before you go to bed, think about a problem you must solve or a creative solution you're in search of. Write down three key words that describe the situation. Focus on those words for a few minutes before you fall asleep. As soon as you wake up, write down or record your thoughts.

NOTES

ACTION STEPS FOR EFFORT

UNFORTUNATELY for all of us, the American dream of working hard and prospering has turned into the American fantasy of getting something for nothing. We want to win the lottery or the publisher's sweepstakes. We've forgotten how much work it takes to earn a living.

Reading this book may inspire you to take action, but it can't do it for you. If you want to achieve your goals, you will need tenacity, persistence, and massive effort. This is where you are put to the test. There are no shortcuts here. There are no allowances for the lazy or complacent. This section will help you understand why, when the going gets tough, there is only one response—effort.

41

Keep moving forward.

My friend Ilene once told me this story about a trip she took to California. She and her friends decided to take a ride to the ocean. Her friends took her to a "secret" cove they knew about where they could have a day of fun in relative privacy. The only problem was that in order to get to the cove, they had to climb down a steep, sandy cliff. Ilene, who was afraid of heights, was not thrilled. But since everyone else was scampering down the cliff and she didn't want to be left standing alone by the side of the highway, Ilene carefully made her way down the hillside.

She and her friends spent several hours in the surf and sun, and had a great time. When it came time to leave, Ilene was nervous about the climb back up the cliff. The pathway seemed even steeper than it had on the way down. She had great difficulty keeping her footing in the loose pebbles and sand. There came a point where Ilene could not find a handhold and her feet kept sliding out from under her. Her friends, already at the top, were shouting encouraging words down to her, but she felt as if she couldn't move.

What choices did she have? She could let herself slide slowly down the hill again, but then where would she be? At the edge of the ocean with the tide coming in! So she had to take action; she could not go backward. She had no other option but to move forward.

"I couldn't look down; that only made me more frightened," says Ilene. "And I couldn't look up; that only made the climb seem so much more impossible to achieve. I had to concentrate only on taking the next step up."

Although her friends had made the climb in about ten minutes, it took Ilene about three-quarters of an hour to get to the top—one tenuous step at a time. Yet, to this day, she feels it was one of her greatest accomplishments. She remembers this climb every time she is in a pressure situation.

"To my friends, climbing that cliff was a piece of cake. I'm sure they never thought about it again," says Ilene. "But to me, it was a life-changing experience. It taught me a great lesson about the limitations we put on ourselves and our abilities (or inabilities) to do certain things. It also taught me about staying in the moment. I knew that the ocean was below me, and I knew that I had to get to the top. But the only way I could get there was to find the next secure handhold and take one more step ahead."

Most of the time, that is all we can do—and all we have to do: take one more step ahead. We can't go back in time. There are no "do-overs" in life. We can only move on from where we are right now; even if the steps are small, each one moves us directly into the future.

42

Learn the action habit.

HUMAN beings are creatures of habit. As much as we'd like to deny that, it's the truth. Taking action is a habit that can be learned and perfected or abused and forgotten. There are people who hardly function at all until they're in a crisis mode. They take action only at the last minute, when they have no choice. They often claim that working in this manner stimulates their creativity; that they're at their best when working under a tight deadline. This may be true for a small percentage of the population, but most of us can't stand the stress that kind of last-minute action puts on our bodies and our minds.

Developing the habit of taking consistent action is like building muscle power. If you wait until two days before a boxing match to get into the ring and train, you're heading for a knockout. However, if you train every day, even only a moderate amount, you have a much better chance of throwing the knockout punch yourself.

You can't wait for the crisis to occur before you take action. If you wait until your bank account is entirely empty before you start to worry about making more money, you'll be out on the street. You can't wait until you have only one client left before you start looking for more prospects. You can't wait until years have gone by before you begin to pursue your dream. You can't wait . . . Well, you get the idea. Taking smart, focused action takes practice, just like everything good in life. So don't wait until something happens before you strengthen your action muscle—start building it bit by bit every day. Then if a crisis should hit, you'll have the strength to deal with it.

When times are slow—it's time for massive action.

THERE are always times in our lives, busy as they may be, when things slow down. There is nothing wrong with taking some of that time to enjoy yourself, to be with friends and family, or perhaps to get some needed rest. But it is also the time to catch up on neglected tasks and to do the little things that are hard to fit in to your daily schedule.

A slow period is a perfect time for correspondence. If you have thank-you notes to send, letters of introduction, or promotional packages that should go out, now is the time to send them. Make phone calls. Especially if you're someone who travels a lot, this is a good time to reduce phone tag. If you can't reach your party, you can leave a message that says exactly when you'll be available for him or her to return your call.

It's the perfect time to write letters, make out a new to-do list, strategize some new projects, think about your goals and whether or not you're on track with them. If you're not, make a list of twenty actions you can take to get back on track again.

When times are good—it's time for massive action.

MY four-year-old son and I were out for a bicycle ride one day. We were going up and down some fairly steep hills (at least for a four-year-old). I told him that if he wanted, he could coast down the hill and not have to keep pedaling. "But Daddy," my son said wisely, "I want to keep pedaling so I can get up the next hill." The things children say, without even realizing the truth behind them!

When things are going well, and the going gets a little easier, we can't afford to coast all the way. We must begin pedaling again so we can get up the next hill. Don't neglect the little things. It's good to do those tasks to fill in the slow times, but don't wait for the slow times to come before you do them. Take advantage of the momentum you've created and do everything you can to keep it going.

Earn the right to claim your accomplishments.

LACK of discipline breaks down self-esteem. We all have days when we can't seem to get anything done. You make a few calls. Write a few pages. Make a stab at getting something done. You don't really want to do anything. Gradually, you start to think you *can't* do anything. Your confidence level sinks and you say to yourself, "I don't deserve success anyway."

Taking action is the cure. Restoring discipline restores self-esteem. Financial genius and billionaire Morty Davis once told me that people who get rich quick, who inherit large sums of money or win the lottery, never appreciate their wealth. They always feel that they have not earned it.

It's only when we have worked hard for something and reached our goal that we can say, "I can claim this success as mine. I have truly earned it." You did all the little things it took to accomplish your goals. You built the relationships, you asked the questions, you made the contacts, you did the follow-up. You separated yourself from the competition. You went overboard and did more than what was expected. You put in the effort and have earned the right to claim what is truly yours.

46

There are two choices in life: You can dig a hole or you can build a mountain. Realize that you're shoveling either way.

No one breezes through life. Everyone does their share of shoveling. What you end up with depends on you. You can focus on the hole you're digging or on the mountain you're building. You can spend your life digging for the buried treasure, chasing after fool's gold, cheating and lying through the day. Or you can use each shovelful to build a solid foundation upon which you can build success. You are constructing your future from the fundamentals you must consistently maintain, the day-to-day tasks that must be accomplished.

The hole represents shortcuts in life, instant gratification, cheating, short-term gains. The mountain represents honesty, effort, fundamentals, long-term gains. All the little things you're doing all the time. When you're constantly digging holes, you'll suddenly find yourself falling into one. Even though it's harder to build a mountain, once you get to the top, you can be proud of what you've accomplished.

When you take the easy way out you will find that you're building tunnels to nowhere that sooner or later will fall in on themselves. When you build a mountain, however, each new shovelful is supported by the one beneath it. Suddenly you find yourself on top of the mountain, and it's huge. People may wonder how you climbed that high. You and you alone know how that mountain was built.

No great thing is created suddenly, any more than a bunch of grapes or a fig. If you tell me that you desire a fig, I answer you that there must be time. Let it first blossom, then bear fruit, then ripen.

EPICTETUS

47

Idle hands are the devil's workshop.

An old saying, but true. Motivational speaker Jim Rohn puts it another way: "Without constant activity, the threats of life will soon overwhelm the values." There are times in your life when the pressure is on, when the stress just keeps building and building. Those are the times you are tempted to take shortcuts. If you are involved in something that you have put your heart and soul into, your values will keep you from giving in to temptation.

Selling is what I do for a living. I know a lot about sales and salespeople. When salespeople have a lot of activity, when they are constantly looking for new leads and following up old ones, when they always have possibilities awaiting them, they are always successful. They don't have to make every single sale, because they know there are plenty of other opportunities down the line.

There is another type of salesperson I see all the time. This person does not have a lot of activity. He's become complacent. He doesn't have very many contacts lined up or leads to follow. He's struggling to make his quota. He's the one who will be tempted to cut corners. He'll resort to a sales pitch like, "I need two more sales to get a trip to Hawaii. Won't you buy something from me just so I can get my trip?" Or he'll drop his price because he's desperate to make the sale. He won't sell the value of his product or company, he'll just sell price.

It's the lack of activity that's causing his downfall. It overwhelms his standards and values. That's why people will grasp on to such get-rich-quick schemes as the lottery, the races, or the casinos. They don't have a lot of activity going on; they're going for things that are out of reach. It's also why kids get into trouble. When there is nothing for them to do, no goals for them to focus on, they get into trouble. They have nothing going on, and nothing lined up for the future. There is nothing for them to attach value to. When you get these kids involved in something—whether it be sports, the arts, community activities—they get out of the streets and on with their lives.

So it is the activity that keeps us on track. When we have something so strong pulling us forward, we hardly see the temptation at all. We don't need the shortcut or the quick fix. We've got better things to do, and better rewards to reap.

48

When you can't fit it in . . . fit it in.

WHEN things are going well, it's hard to fit things in—phone calls you should make, people you should write to, meetings you should attend. It's too easy to get complacent. It's too easy to coast on your good fortune and not put in the extra effort that led to your success in the first place. But it's when things are rolling along that you need the extra effort even more.

When you think everything is going smoothly, when it seems that you've got everything in place, that's the time to step back and say, "Where can I add just one more hour?" "What one more thing can I do to guarantee things keep moving forward?" You never know when that one more hour you put in may turn into a week's, a month's, or a year's worth of new business. It usually turns out that the small sacrifices you make come back to you in ways you could never imagine.

49

Try being an early bird.

I constantly tell people to stay at work one hour later than usual. You'd be amazed at how many other people are doing the same, and you can often catch people at their desks when the phones have stopped ringing and most of the office has gone home.

But you might also want to try starting early. I called someone recently to set up an appointment. I asked, "What's the earliest I can see you?" He replied, "I start my day at six-thirty. Are you free then?" Normally, I'm more of a night person and six-thirty is a little early. But I realized that if I really wanted to see this man, I had to accommodate myself to his schedule. So I said, "Sure."

You'll find that many successful people start early. Just think about it: If you start work at seven, you have a two-hour jump on the rest of the world. Next time you complain about not having enough hours in the day, try starting earlier.

50

Lick the envelopes yourself.

THERE are times when it pays to do something yourself, the old-fashioned, time-consuming way. Occasionally when I have a large mailing that needs to go out, instead of having the printer fold, staple, and stuff, I'll do it myself. This gives me time to think and strategize. I visualize what I'd like this mailing to accomplish. I add personal notes to some people. I make mental connections and form strategic moves for when I get back to my desk. I make a list of those people I will follow up with another mailing, or perhaps a phone call. The mindless acts of stuffing and stamping give me the time and freedom for the creative thinking I can't always do under pressure situations.

Of course, there is something to be said for delegation. There are times when I can't take the time to do this kind of manual labor myself. But when I can, I do. I recently had my back deck rebuilt. I hired experts to do it, but I helped. I dug holes for the foundation, sawed wood, and pounded nails. I got a sore back and some blisters. But now when I sit outside on that deck, I enjoy it so much more. I've earned the right to enjoy it.

That's why the best way to be successful in business is to start from the bottom up. To know all the hard work, labor, and pain that goes into building something. There is no substitute for the knowledge and satisfaction you gain from participating in something from the ground up. Every great leader is involved with the troops. Every great manager goes out into the field and meets customers. They know the valuable lessons to be learned, and they know that they have now earned the right to lead.

51

Make a decision and go with it.

IN today's world, everything has become extremely complex. Take the computer, for instance. It was invented in order to speed up and improve the processing of documents and data. In some respects, it has done that. But in other respects, it has slowed us down. We now have about three hundred times more information available to us than we did only a few years ago. And sometimes all that information is more confusing than useful. We become paralyzed because it's so hard to decide the right thing to do.

Jim Ivy, CEO of Savin Corporation, believes that many people have let business become too complex. "We do this because we think we're sophisticated," he says, "or we're manipulating the market, or we think we're doing a better job of servicing our customers. But in reality we've made life too complex for our customers and for our own employees. We bog actions down by trying to be more complex than we need to be. And by spending too much time analyzing too much data."

Ivy has a system for implementing decisions within his company. He calls a meeting and sets the problem before his staff. They then identify two or three alternative actions they can take to solve the problem. "Then we force ourselves to choose one," he says. "I refuse to leave a meeting unless we have picked a course of action." That plan is then implemented. "And," adds Ivy, "we always learn more from implementing an action than we ever would have trying to figure out which was the 'best' course of action to take. The implementation guides you on how to make critical adjustments, how to change directions slightly in order to have the action be successful."

That's not to say every decision turns out to be the best. Sometimes Ivy finds that the plan is not working. By that time, he knows why it's not working, and he knows what to do to succeed with the next plan.

Sometimes it's better to just shoot than to stop and aim.

A man is driving down the street. He sees a house on fire down the block. He pulls the car over, jumps out, and runs into the burning house. He saves the two small children inside. Afterward he is asked, "How did you know what to do?" "I didn't," he replies. "I didn't think about it, I just did it." If he had stopped to think, two children's lives might have been lost.

Sometimes problems loom large in front of us. We delay taking action because we want to be sure we understand the problem thoroughly and that we have analyzed every possible solution. By that time, however, the problem has totally engulfed us.

"I'm inclined to think that what you want to do is make sure you've got bullets in your gun, make sure that you can see the target, and then point and fire," says Savin's Jim Ivy. "Then adjust and fire, adjust and fire, adjust and fire." He compares the situation to Godzilla about to destroy your town. It's a big, clear target and you've got to take him down. Your best bet is to start firing and keep firing until you come up with a better solution.

"A lot of problems we deal with are almost as big as Godzilla," says Ivy. "I don't think you need to spend four or five days aiming before you shoot. You start firing first, then you adjust your aim."

53

Maintain quality in everything you do.

EVERY action you take must have the highest standard of quality in it. Don't rush through tasks just to get them done. Don't say, "No one will notice; this doesn't have to be so great." First of all, you never know who just might notice. Wouldn't you rather someone noticed the excellent job you did, instead of commenting on your sloppiness? Secondly, value your own work. Take pride in what you do. I've heard many people stand up proudly after a job well done and say, "I worked hard to get this done." I've never heard anyone stand up proudly and say, "I cut corners to get here."

No one is perfect all the time. You should not demand perfection from yourself or from others around you. But you can strive for it. You will make mistakes. But the actions you take in good faith, those with 100 percent effort behind them, will hold up in the end. They will build upon each other and give you the strong footing you need to climb to even greater heights.

54

Concentrate on the task at hand.

STAY in the moment. Think about what you have to accomplish at the moment you're doing it. We make mistakes when we lose concentration, when we let our minds drift away and stop paying attention. You can reflect upon the past and dream about the future when the project is completed, but while it's under way, keep your focus sharp and to the point.

If you find that difficult to do, if you can't give 110 percent to the actions you're taking, you need to reevaluate your purpose. Is this something you really should be doing? Is it moving you toward your goal, or away from it? Is there some better, more efficient way to get this task accomplished? Once you've come up with answers to those questions, you can reestablish your concentration and once again focus on your current activity.

Concentration and attention also allow you to go beneath the surface, to reach the depth you must in order to truly understand what you're doing. You are immersed in the people and situation around you. When your attention drifts, you stop listening to people, you make errors in judgment, you lose sight of your goals. When your concentration is strong, however, you are so focused that nothing can distract you from your task.

Even if our efforts of attention seem for years to be producing no result, one day a light that is in exact proportion to them will flood the soul.

SIMONE WEIL

Create a sense of urgency.

SUCCESSFUL people always have a sense of urgency about things that have to be done. Without that sense of urgency, there's an open invitation for procrastination to slip in. When a task becomes less important, it's easy to say, "I'll do it tomorrow."

It was my dream to get my friend and superstar sports agent Marc Roberts to write a book. He's taught me many lessons in life, and I knew he had a lot to teach others as well. But when I started sending out his book proposal through my literary agency, we received many rejections. It seems that other sports agents have written books, and many of the recent ones sat on the shelves and didn't sell very well. Publishers were reluctant to try again.

It got to a point where I had a decision to make. I could listen to the publishers' rejections, or I could make an all-out push to sell the book. I took a hint from the film *Apollo 13* and told myself, "Failure is not an option." I created a sense of urgency. This book was going to be sold, and it was going to be sold soon. I had faith in Marc Roberts and faith in the book. I made an even greater effort than I had before, and within two weeks the book was sold.

What had changed? The sense of urgency not only renewed my faith and excitement about the book, it helped me communicate that to the people I approached.

Accomplish the small but difficult tasks and great things will happen without effort.

SOMETIMES the greatest challenges we face in life are the smallest. The tiniest detail can be the thing that makes the difference between success and failure. The more you do when you have the chance—when you're not under pressure or under the gun—the greater the chances that you'll be prepared when the big things come along.

For instance, I give speeches and seminars around the country. Many small steps are necessary in preparing for these events. Some things I can prepare way ahead of time. The more I can do beforehand, the less I have to worry about as the event approaches. I need to concentrate on my presentation, not whether or not all my materials have been prepared. If everything has been done, I can set off for my speech with confidence. The delivery is solid, based on the foundation of thorough preparation.

Without the preparation, the foundation is shaky. You can't concentrate on the presentation, all you can do is worry about how you will get everything completed on time and whether or not you have everything you need. The audience can sense your discomfort and they feel as nervous as you do.

Take care of the small things and the big things will take care of themselves. Other people may only see the big thing, but you will know about how much you did to make it happen. You will have the satisfaction of knowing that each small detail was a major contribution to your success.

The most successful men in the end are those whose success is the result of steady accretion. . . . It is the man who carefully advances step by step, with his mind becoming wider and wider—and progressively better able to grasp any theme or situation—persevering in what he knows to be practical, and concentrating his thought upon it, who is bound to succeed in the greatest degree.

ALEXANDER GRAHAM BELL

57

Experience total exhaustion—and beyond.

SOME tasks require extraordinary effort. When these occasions arise, it's time to go all out. Go past your barriers. Go past the point where you want to give up and fall asleep. Push yourself. You'll be surprised by what you can accomplish. Many times, once you defy the strong temptation to give in and give up, you get a second wind that keeps you going far beyond what you thought you could do. You see that you have more to give.

Dr. Phil Santiago, official chiropractor to U.S. Olympic athletes, was at the Olympic trials in 1996 when Michael Johnson earned his reputation as the fastest human on earth. Santiago was impressed and amazed by both Johnson's attitude and his willingness to do whatever it took to win the gold and break the world record. During the trials, Santiago asked Johnson how he was feeling. "Fine," the athlete replied. "I'm going to break the world record today." He did—but there was a technical problem with the timer and the officials would not count that race. Afterward, Santiago commiserated with Johnson on his bad luck. "No problem," Johnson replied. "I'll break it again tomorrow." And he did.

Johnson also had the opportunity to win four gold medals in the games. He qualified to run the relays as well as the individual two-hundred-meter race. But he was so focused on destroying the Olympic and world records, he didn't care about winning the rest of the medals. "He selected the goal he wanted," says Santiago. "He knew that in order to break these records, he'd probably rip his muscles and be unable to run the relays. That was okay with him." And that's what happened. Immediately after the race, his legs were packed in ice and he was out of commission for a week and a half. He'd known that would happen, but he had the discipline and the focus, the mental strength to go even beyond his body's limits.

Now, I am not recommending that you go to the extreme of ripping your muscles in order to reach your goal. I am recommending that you go beyond the point where you think you must stop. If Michael Johnson had not done that, the old world speed record would still be standing. It is amazing what we can do when we let go of the limitations we put on ourselves. If you want something hard enough, and you focus on it well enough, you can accomplish anything.

58

Discover the rewards of taking risks.

MANY of the actions we take are difficult but not particularly scary. Other actions are not particularly difficult, but may be incredibly frightening. Of course, frightening is a relative term. If you're an outgoing person who loves to get up and entertain, making a business presentation may be just another part of the job. But if you're shy and don't like speaking in public, that same presentation may send shivers up your spine. To you, taking that action may appear to be a great risk (What if you forget what you're supposed to say? What if you have a coughing fit in the middle? What if your boss doesn't like it?)

But if you don't take the risk, you can't reap the reward. When you take an action that includes some degree of fear behind it, you automatically increase your confidence level. You know that you have gone beyond your fear, that you have made the effort. And if you can do it once, you can do it again—and you can move on to the next level of action.

Each level of action we achieve serves as the foundation for the one to follow. If there are any cracks in that foundation, they are filled in every time you take a risk and move past it. You can't live in a foundation. You have to build the house. And the only way you can build that house is to work through your fears, take the necessary risks, and reap the great rewards.

59

Make more from less.

ALBERT Einstein devised three rules of work:

1. Out of clutter, find simplicity.

2. From discord, find harmony.

3. In the middle of difficulty lies opportunity.

When you are in the middle of an intense project that requires massive activity, think about ways to simplify what you're doing. Perhaps you can combine some steps. Perhaps you can get advice from someone who's been down this path before. Whenever someone says, "There must be an easier way to do this," they're usually right. When everything around you is going crazy, take the time to stop, look around, and find the harmony. Find the balance. Look for the humor. Have the patience to notice the light at the end of the tunnel. If you can find the harmony within yourself, you can pass your calm confidence on to others around you. And remember that there are lessons to be learned from even the worst adversity. Where there's a major difficulty, find the opportunity in it.

60

Strive for the "Being of Nothingness."

LEONARDO da Vinci said, "Among the great things that are to be found among us, the Being of Nothingness is the greatest." The Being of Nothingness means to let yourself go, to be part of nature. The Being of Nothingness is difficult to achieve, because as soon as you strive for it, it's lost. That's the paradox, the yin and the yang. You want to find it without looking for it. Only by taking action can it be achieved, but action that is pure and truthful. It is the Zen philosophy of the archer being one with the arrow, of finding peace and solitude in the middle of the bizarre realities of life.

When you are true to yourself, when you take action with a purposeful direction, when you are in the midst of life and enjoying every part of it, then you can achieve the Being of Nothingness.

61

Live by this word: "today."

PUT the word "today" in bold lettering somewhere you can see it easily. It's a good reminder of so many different things:

- It means that this minute is the most important time you'll ever have. You'll never get this block of time back again. For all you know, that's all there is.

- You can't relive the past. If you focus on what once was, it reduces your ability to take action right now.

- It's good to visualize the future, but if you focus all your energy on what might happen, you're less likely to do what you have to do right now.

- "Today" is a reminder not to procrastinate. It's so easy to put things off. There are many things we'd rather be doing than the tasks we have to perform. According to Rick Warren of the Oklahoma City Christian Business Men's Committee, procrastination comes in eight phases:

Phase 1—Hopeful: *"I'll start early this time."*
Phase 2—Tension: *"I've got to start soon."*
Phase 3—Creeping guilt: *"I should have started sooner."*
Phase 4—False reassurance: *"There is still time to do it."*
Phase 5—Desperation: *"What's wrong with me?"*
Phase 6—Intense pain: *"I can't wait any longer!"*
Phase 7—Get it over with: *"Just get it done."*
Phase 8—The cycle repeats: *"Next time, I'll start earlier."*

Procrastination is a devious enemy. It is addictive. It quickly becomes a habit that is difficult to break. Hanging the word "today" in plain view can help you avoid this self-destructive behavior that procrastination engenders.

"Today" can help spur you into action in another way. Think about who you are today versus the person you were ten years, five years, six months ago. You have learned so much during that time. Your view of the world has changed. Your experiences have made you a different person.

But realize that the reason you are where you are today is because of all the things you did ten years ago. Know that everything you've learned in those ten years makes you that much more prepared for success. Think about how much more you know now than you did then. When I look back just a few years ago, I see how I was preparing myself for today. I started doing a radio show knowing nothing about the industry. If I hadn't done that show, I would never have learned, would never have made the incredible contacts I made. Those experiences enable me to do my television show today. Who knows what this television show will enable me to do five years from now?

Today is the day to try something new, something you may be scared to try. Today is the day to meet new people. Today is the day to take a new action. You never know which action you take is the one you'll look back on ten years from now, saying, "That is the action that got me here." Today is the day you can take that one step forward that just may change your life.

———————

In this very breath we take now lies the secret that all great teachers try to tell us.

PETER MATTHIESSEN

62

Leave them laughing or leave them in the dust.

COMEDIANS always say that you should leave your audience laughing. But we're not all comedians, and we can't always end with a laugh. So if you can't leave them laughing, the next best thing is to leave them in the dust. Jerry Seinfeld did both—he ended his series with a funny final episode while he was at the height of his popularity. People will always remember him as a successful TV actor. The moral of the story: In whatever you do, finish strong.

What people remember most about you is often what you did last. This is as important in my business as in any other. I was in Chicago recently to give a seminar. Several of the managers were getting together for a friendly game of basketball before the day's activities, and they invited me to join the game. I hadn't played in a while. I was running up and down the court and, after a short time, I felt like I needed an oxygen mask and a back brace. Finally, I sat on the bench to get my breath. I came back in for the last few seconds of the game, which my team won. Although everybody was jumping up and down and high-fiving, I felt guilty because I only played for the last minute. While everybody else was sweating and huffing and puffing, I had just come off the bench.

Another game started up and I was determined to give it my all. Somehow, I made some amazing moves to the hoop. I made up for my earlier performance. Now I could go into the seminar knowing that these managers would remember me as a player willing to give his all to the game. That's your goal—you want people to remember you as a player willing to give your all to the game and finish strong.

63

The pain of discipline is easier to endure than the pain of regret.

THERE is nothing worse than looking back on your life and saying, "I wish I had done this, had taken this risk, had grabbed that opportunity." The pain of regret can be truly agonizing. The pain of discipline—making yourself do something you don't want to do—is nothing in comparison. It is temporary. When the task is completed, the pain disappears. But we live with regret for the rest of our lives.

Ten years from now, you'll be proud of the hard work you're doing now. "Yes," you will say, "it was difficult. I put in long hours. I endured discomfort and inconvenience. But I made it through and reached my goal." So remind yourself as you're putting in those extra hours, when you're taking the necessary actions and completing the fundamentals, when you're tempted to give up and go home—remind yourself that you never want to look back ten years from now and say, "If only . . ." Those are the two saddest words in the English language.

SUMMARY

- Keep moving forward. When times are rough, there is only one thing to do: take one small step ahead. There is no point in reliving failures, or trying to accomplish a goal in one fell swoop. The only solution is to move on, one step at a time.

- Taking action is a habit that can be learned and perfected. Don't wait for a crisis to occur before you take action; if your action "muscle" is out of shape, it won't serve you when you need it.

- When times are slow, it's time for massive action. When times are good, it's time for massive action. In other words, it's always time for action!

- Restoring discipline restores self-esteem. It's only when you have worked hard for success, when you have truly earned your rewards, that you have earned the right to claim your accomplishments.

- Activity keeps us on track. Idleness leads to boredom, boredom leads to complacency, and complacency leads to failure. Lack of activity often leads you into the temptation of looking for shortcuts—get-rich-quick schemes, implausible dreams, and even illegal activities. When we have goals and specific tasks to achieve, they pull us forward and away from temptation.

- Valuable lessons can be learned from participating in every aspect of your job. Many of the most successful executives started from the ground up. Along the way they learned everything there was to know about their business. They also know that they earned the right to the position they now hold.

- Make a decision and go with it. With so much informational input available to us, it's often hard to decide which option is the best one to take. There are times when it is best to make any decision than to try and guess which one will produce perfect results. Even if the action you take turns out to be a mistake, you can learn from your error and go on to take a more productive route.

- Value your own work and take pride in what you do. Don't think that no one will notice if you don't do your best. Even if no one else sees, you will know the difference.

- Pay attention to what you're doing. Stay in the moment. You can plan for the future, but you can only *do* right now. If you let your attention wander, what you are doing right now will suffer. When you lose concentration, you lose sight of your goals. When you remain focused, nothing can distract you from your task.

- Meet the smallest challenge, and the biggest will take care of itself. Every great undertaking is made of small tasks that must be accomplished. Once all of these small challenges have been met, the great undertaking has been miraculously achieved!

- Every level of action we achieve serves as the foundation for the one to follow. If you never take any risks or try anything new, you will stay at the same low level of existence. But every time you put in the effort, you build your foundation higher, move on to the next level, and reap your well-deserved rewards.

- "If only" are the two saddest words in the English language. It isn't the things we've tried that we regret, but the chances we never took.

ACTION PLANS

- Every day, take one action that requires risk or effort. That doesn't mean jumping out of a plane or lifting a boulder. Risk and effort are relative terms. It can be risky to make a phone call that might end in rejection. For some people, it may take a major effort to cook a healthy meal or get out and exercise. However you define the terms, set yourself a task that is beyond your usual boundaries, then accomplish it.

- When things are going well, keep them going longer. Add one extra phone call, one more e-mail or piece of correspondence, or one more hour's work, into your day. You never know which one of the added efforts will pay off in spades.

- One day a week, start your day an hour earlier. See how much you can accomplish by starting your day at seven instead of eight, or eight instead of nine. If you find your body rhythm changing to accommodate this earlier start, move up to two days of early starts, then three, then four and so on.

- Every once in a while, do a job you would normally delegate to someone else. Do some manual labor, or a menial job you would normally hire someone to do for you. Use the time to plan and strategize, to free yourself for some creative thinking.

- When a task is extremely important to you, go to extreme measures. Pull out the stops and go beyond your barriers. Push yourself until you get your second wind. If you go beyond the point where you think you must stop, you'll often find you can accomplish much more than you thought you could. There are many limitations we place on ourselves—limitations that are not based on reality. The only way to find out what we can actually accomplish is to push the envelope and astound ourselves.

- Hang the word "TODAY" somewhere where you can see it easily. Procrastination is a difficult habit to break. The word "today" can spur you into action when you need it most.

NOTES

ACTION STEPS FOR ADDING VALUE

THERE are many ways to move things forward. One of the best ways is to take an action that not only is well researched and well planned, but also helps others besides yourself. The most powerful actions, and the ones that push you ahead the fastest, are those that benefit others. So not only does your action move you toward your goal, it adds value to others' lives and comes back to reward you another day. It's the "one plus one equals three" factor.

Every time you take an action, you should be thinking about its impact. Who does it affect, and how does it affect them? If it is going to be harmful, it should obviously be avoided. If it is going to be beneficial, then try to think of ways to spread the benefits around. Although it's been said a thousand times before, this sentiment bears repeating: Our rewards in life are in direct proportion to our service. When you take an action that benefits others, you're not only helping them, you're building leverage for yourself as well. Now you're not working alone toward your goal, you've got all those you have helped on your side and willing to help you when you need it.

64

Attack with value from all sides.

THIS is a way of building value into every action you take. It is another visual aid for planning, like the spiderweb. This graphic, however, is a circle. I use it often when I'm selling. My customer is the center of the circle. On the outside of the circle I put all the things that will give that customer added value, the benefits that differentiate me from the competition. Then when I'm ready to meet the customer, I know I've got him surrounded with value, and I can come from any direction with a benefit that will keep him within the circle of my sale.

This method can be applied to any project or action. Place your objective in the center of the circle. Then start plotting things on the outside of that circle that can bring value to the centerpiece.

65

Build leverage with respect for others.

ONE way to keep ourselves moving forward, especially when we are feeling bogged down in details, is to change the focus from ourselves to others. When we get so caught up in ourselves and our own plans for glory, we lose our objectivity. Instead of moving forward, we're moving around in circles.

My background is in sales, and I have taught thousands of other salespeople in my seminars and workshops. The unsuccessful salesperson is one who keeps only his goal in mind—to sell the product. He doesn't care who buys his product, or why. He only wants to make sure he meets his quota. This kind of salesperson may have short bursts of success, but won't be able to keep it up in the long run.

The successful salesperson, on the other hand, focuses on the needs of his customers. He learns as much as he possibly can about the goals and objectives of the other person, and then identifies the ways he (and his product or service) can best serve those needs. That is the salesperson who will create long-lasting relationships and long-term success.

Everyone is a salesperson to one degree or another. If you're not selling an actual product or service, you're selling your ideas to others. Whatever you're selling, people won't buy from you because you need to make a sale. They buy because there is some connection between what you're selling and something that's missing in their lives, and what you have to offer will fill that gap. When you sell with other people's needs in mind, you're building leverage for future sales.

Building leverage is important in every aspect of your life. I got a call last week from a business acquaintance. He is in a fairly high-level position, but felt that his job was going nowhere. He was at the point where he wanted to "try something different," even if he wasn't quite sure what that would be. He was calling to ask for my advice.

I told him that the best thing he could do for himself right now was to look for ways he could better meet the needs of his current employer—do the best possible job he could do in his current position—and make himself invaluable to the company. I suggested he concentrate on making every project he worked on a huge success. Once that happened, he would increase his worth to the company and be in a much better position to request a higher salary from his current employer or to look for a job somewhere else. He would be able to walk away with confidence and a track record that breeds success.

Two things happen with this kind of leverage building. When my friend first called, his focus was solely on his dissatisfaction with his job. Once he started focusing on meeting the company's needs, he not only created added value for himself, he also lifted himself out of the doldrums and refueled his personal energy system.

It is this kind of outward focus that keeps Val-Pak's Joe Bourdow motivated. He started out as a franchisee with a staff of three. Now, as president of the company, he oversees more than twenty-five hundred people.

"I'm responsible for these people," says Bourdow. "I want to make sure we're doing everything possible for our advertisers and everyone who works at Val-Pak. That means making sure we're putting out the best possible product for our sales representative to offer local advertisers. I have to be sure that this whole enterprise works, but I do it on behalf of all the other people involved. It's a lot of responsibility and I take it very seriously. My job is to work for them."

He is the richest man who enriches his country most; in whom the people feel richest and proudest; who gives himself with his money; who opens the doors of opportunity widest to those about him; who is ears to the deaf, eyes to the blind, and feet to the lame. Such a man makes every acre of land in his community worth more, and makes richer every man who lives near him.

ORISON SWETT MARDEN

66

Do more than you're paid to do.

THERE are people who do their job, do what they're supposed to do, and do it reasonably well. Then there are people who take pride in their job, who go beyond their job description and provide exceptional service. They don't do it because they expect an immediate reward for it, but they do know that they will benefit down the road.

People notice when you give more than is expected. When you go into a restaurant, for example, who gets the bigger tip—the waitress who simply takes your order and serves your food, or the one who points out the best items on the menu, recommends a good wine to go with your dinner, and brings you a small taste of the dessert you couldn't decide whether or not to order? Of course, the second waitress will get a generous tip because she added to your enjoyment of the dining experience.

Recently, I had a painter come and do some odd jobs around my house. We agreed upon a price, and he did everything I asked—and more. He saw some things that I had missed, and he repaired and repainted them. He did not expect any more money; he saw it as part of doing a good job. Now I recommend him to every homeowner I know. Who knows how many more clients he will get because of his extraordinary service to me.

It doesn't matter what occupation or field you're in. You will always come across opportunities to do more than is expected of you. You can choose to ignore them, or you can choose to make a habit of providing exceptional value. You never know who might be watching.

67

Do not judge an action by its size, but by its impact.

If you think that no one will notice the little things you do, you're wrong. If you think that no one will notice the little things you don't do, you're wrong as well. You never know who's watching.

If you do only what is asked or expected, you may accomplish your goal. But if you do more, if you do it because you believe in it, because you're passionate about it, because it's the right thing to do . . . your rewards will be that much more intense.

The Japanese philosopher Shunryu Suzuki said, "Zen is not some kind of excitement, but concentration on our usual everyday routine." If you want to get the most out of life, you have to put the most into it. It's the little things you do that count. You never know what thing it is that will have the most impact on other people. One act of kindness can change someone's life. When you're gone, the people you've affected will carry part of you with them. You leave your lessons alive in the people who remember you. It's a wonderful feeling knowing that you can make a difference in people's lives every day. So make every action count—the littlest one may be the one with the greatest impact.

68

Create a tidal wave of support for your goals and objectives.

BUILDING relationships is one of the most powerful tools you possess for realizing your dreams. It's almost impossible to reach your goals alone. There are many people along the way who can help. It's important to build as many solid relationships as you can with people at all levels, from the receptionist to the VP to the CEO. Treat everyone you speak to with respect and good humor and they will support you when it counts. Know that each person with whom you establish rapport is a link in the chain that will eventually lead you right to your goal.

When you get someone excited about your goals—especially when you can tie what you're doing together with what they're doing—you're building leverage for success. You're actually creating your own sales force of people who will promote your message as well as their own. And the more value you build for them, the more they're going to support you.

What goes around comes around. If your actions benefit others, they will benefit you as well. It's impossible to be of service to everyone, so choose places where you will have the greatest impact. In that way, the greatest payback will come to you. When you input so much value into a relationship, you earn the right to ask for the support.

69

Build a mountain of continued effort and value.

Iт is the small, concentrated movements that get us to our goals. Only by taking these small actions can we complete the large one. That's why we need to focus on every single step, no matter how small or tedious. That's why we need to keep going, even when (and especially when) we think we're not getting anywhere. It's easy to get bogged down in the feeling that nothing is being accomplished. When we understand that it's the small things that build great value, we can use that knowledge to keep forging ahead.

From time to time, for instance, I sit down with a tape recorder and dictate twenty or thirty letters to various clients and colleagues. They may be people I'd like to do business with, people I need to send follow-up letters or packets or materials to, or people I just want to stay in touch with—there are dozens of reasons for writing. But this is the kind of task that is difficult to accomplish during the workday when the phones are ringing, I have meetings to attend, or I'm out of town giving seminars. So it's usually late at night or on the weekends when I'm dictating these letters.

By the time I've finished, I feel relieved and energized at the same time. After making contact with all these people and generating that kind of exposure, it adds a new level to my mountain of continued effort for that day. And, since I always include some kind of benefit for the other person in my letter (a networking contact, a piece of information he needs, an article of interest to her), I know that I've done something of value for the people who receive these letters.

Sometimes it's easier to get our juices flowing when we have reached a crisis—when we run into an obstacle or experience unexpected failure. It's the day-to-day drudgery that often gets us down. It's the routine tasks that sap our energy and make us complacent. That's when it's time to dig deeper, to ask yourself, "Am I doing everything I can to reach my goal?" Sometimes the answer is that you just have to keep going with the small stuff. If part of reaching your goal requires you to do a mailing to two thousand people, you can't stop at eight hundred because it's boring and you feel you should be doing something more exciting. The mailing must be completed.

On the other hand, there may be other steps that can be taken while the mailing is completed. Have you put a follow-up plan in place? Do you know what you are going to do if two hundred people respond? if two thousand people respond? Often, you can get some of your best thinking done while performing mundane, but necessary, tasks.

70

Make people feel important and they'll move your actions forward farther and faster.

It's amazing what we sometimes do to manipulate other people. Often we're not even aware of what we're doing. What we want is help from other people, and what we end up doing is alienating them.

Lots of people start off conversations that way. They want to impress the other party with how much they know (or think they know). They say things like, "I've been around. I know what I want and I know how you should do your job. Let me tell you how to do this." They think they're gaining credibility by showing off their expertise, but just the opposite is happening.

If you want someone's help, you must let him know you respect and admire his abilities. You want him to become your partner, not your adversary. You can say, "I've seen your work and it's terrific. I'm sure I can learn a lot from you. This is what I need to have done. Is there anything I can do to help you do your job?"

You can take this attitude no matter who you're speaking to—your employee, your spouse, your children. When something is very important to you, when you're excited about something and want to make sure it comes out well, it's only natural to want to retain control of the situation. You want to set the stage at the very beginning so that everything else follows smoothly. But there are times where you have to let someone else do what he or she does best. When you acknowledge someone else's abilities and expertise, you make that person feel important. You give the person recognition, which is something every human being craves. And when that happens, people catch your excitement. They will want to prove that you were right to place your faith in them, and they, too, will want the best possible result.

71

Enjoy the process, not just the goal.

At the age of twenty-two, Hal Becker became Xerox Corporation's top salesperson out of a sales force of eleven thousand people. At the age of twenty-seven, he founded Direct Opinions to help companies in various industries achieve customer satisfaction through telemarketing. And at the age of twenty-eight, he was diagnosed with terminal cancer. Surviving that experience has given Becker a very special view of life.

"The best thing that ever happened to me was having terminal cancer," says Becker. "Now, I have a picture that I carry around with me of when I was down to eighty-three pounds. So when I have a bad day, if I have a problem in my life or an argument with a client, I look at that picture and I say, 'This is not a bad day.'

"You have to appreciate how lucky you are, that you are able to go after the things you want. There's an old saying that goes, The harder you work, the luckier you get. In business, if you strike out seven out of ten times that's failure. In baseball, that's three million dollars a year. So I'm going to get to bat as many times as I can every day.

"People sometimes ask me, 'What's the biggest mistake you ever made?' I make mistakes every day. But I enjoy what I'm doing, and I go after my goals little by little. I take each day one at a time. I look for things that make me happy, and the ones that don't, I let them go and move on. If I get upset, I change the situation. If I can't change the situation, I change my attitude and move on to something else."

This sentiment is echoed by opera singer Judith Von Houser. She studies, practices, and rehearses six days a week. One of the most difficult things she has had to learn in her career was not musical technique. It was to learn to enjoy the process. "You always want to get to the end and you're miserable if you're not there," she says. "What if I never get to my goal? Does that mean that all those years of practice and study were for nothing? Of course not. You learn valuable lessons all along the way. Too many people say, 'Once I get there I'll be happy.' That just isn't true. If you're not happy along the way, you won't be happy 'there' either."

It is good to have an end to journey toward; but it is the journey that matters, in the end.

URSULA K. LE GUIN

72

Appreciate the gifts you are given.

THERE is such a thing in life as serendipity—when we are unexpectedly lucky, when we are at the right place at the right time. This only happens a few times in life. Those people who achieve success recognize that they are in the right place and are willing to take advantage of any opportunity they might find there. They know that they have been given a gift, but it is up to them to use it well.

We don't know when our gifts will run out. Therefore, we have an obligation to appreciate whatever we have. Every day is a gift and we must treat it as the special gift it is. We never know how many days we have. Several years ago, Dr. Fred Epstein had a fourteen-year-old patient who had already undergone several operations for brain tumors. Her prognosis was not good. She was scheduled for one more operation, which would not cure her but might prolong her life. She had to make a choice as to whether or not she wanted to undergo another grueling operation.

"If you do this operation," she asked Dr. Epstein, "will I live through the summer?"

"Yes," he replied.

"Then do it," she said. "Give me the summer."

Dr. Epstein and his team performed the delicate operation. She lived to see the summer flowers bloom, and she loved every day she had left to her. She died in the fall, but she taught everyone who knew her a lesson about appreciating the time you have. It is to be treasured and prized. There is no excuse for wasting the gifts you have been given—your talents, your skills, your friends and family, and the opportunities that come your way.

College is the last period of time that will seem lengthy to you at only three or four years. From now on, time will pass without artificial academic measure. It will go by like the wind. Whatever you want to do, do it now. For life is time, and time is all there is.

GLORIA STEINEM

SUMMARY

- The most powerful actions, the ones that push you forward, are those that impact others. They add value to others' lives, and come back to reward you another day.

- Everyone is a salesperson, whether you're selling an actual product or service, or selling your ideas to others. People will only buy from you if what you have to offer matches up with a need they have in their lives. When you sell with other people's needs in mind, you're building leverage for future sales.

- Take every opportunity you can to do more than is expected of you. Make a habit of providing exceptional value. You never know who is watching, and you never know what rewards you might reap because of your extra effort.

- The littlest action may be the one with the greatest impact. Every action you take has a ripple effect. It impacts people and situations way beyond your sight. You may never know the impact your action has—but it just may change someone's life. Don't you want that life-changing action to be one that you're proud of?

- It's almost impossible to realize your dreams and reach your goals alone. It's important to build as many solid relationships as you can along the way. Treat everyone with respect and good humor. Each person with whom you interact is a link in the chain that will eventually lead you to your goal.

- Make everyone you meet feel important. If you want someone's help, you must let him know you respect and admire his abilities.

Give them recognition—something every human being craves. You will gain respect and admiration—and support—in return.

- Enjoy the process, not just the goal. Life is a journey, and that journey is short. If you're forever waiting—waiting to be successful, waiting to be rich, waiting to be happy—you may never be any of those things. If you're so focused on achieving your goals that you can't enjoy your life in the present moment, then those goals are worthless. It always comes back to the yin and yang—striving toward your goals, yet still taking the time to experience inner peace and harmony.

ACTION PLANS

- Every time you take an action, think about its impact. Who might it affect? How might it affect them? If it is potentially harmful, what other action can you take instead? If it is potentially beneficial, how can you spread the benefits around?

- Construct a graphic representation of your objective and the value you bring to it. Draw a circle. Place your objective in the center of the circle. All along the perimeter of the circle, plot the benefits that will bring value to the center piece.

- If you find yourself in a rut, or unable to decide how to solve a problem, shift your focus away from yourself and toward others. Focus on meeting other people's needs and you will find yourself refueled and reenergized.

- Get other people excited about your goals. Figure out how your goals can benefit them and they will automatically become part of your support team. When you bring value to the relationship, you earn the right to ask for help.

ACTION STEPS FOR ENERGY

WITHOUT energy, there can be no action. Energy determines how you move forward physically, mentally, and emotionally. It governs what you do and how you do it. Most of the time we take energy for granted. We think of it when we're running low on fuel, when we haven't taken proper care of ourselves and we feel we are not up to the tasks ahead. These action steps will help you understand how to find the reserves of your untapped energy, how to use it to your greatest personal benefit.

We are all living organisms here on this planet. Life is fragile and life is short. It is too short and precious to have our minds and bodies not functioning at optimal performance levels. We must be aware of what we eat, what we drink, who we're with, and how we think. We can learn to harness our mental, physical, and spiritual energy to keep us motivated and inspired. It will allow us not only to take more actions, but to make those actions more powerful and vibrant.

73

Energy creates action; action creates energy.

Here's the good news about action and energy: The more action you take, the more energy you have. The more energy you create, the more actions you can take. The two feed off each other. We've all experienced this phenomenon. It's very difficult to *think* your way out of a state of low energy. It's much easier to get out of it by *doing* something. Just looking at your desk piled high with work can make you feel exhausted. It's so easy just to say, "I don't feel like getting this work done today. I don't have the energy." Once you say that, it's true. You won't get the work done today, and tomorrow it will still be there, right where you left it.

If you look at the pile on the desk and say, "I don't feel like getting this work done today. However, I'll just do one thing and then I'll stop." Guess what happens? You do one thing—but you don't stop. Then you do one more thing, then you do another and another, and before you know it, you've made considerable headway toward getting the job done. Even if you don't finish it today, you've got much less to do tomorrow.

The reason for this is reflected in the laws of physics having to do with inertia and momentum. Inertia is when "matter retains its state of rest as long as it is not acted upon by an outside force." Your energy state will remain at a low level unless it is acted upon by an outside force—in other words, once you take an action, you start the ball rolling. That's when momentum comes in. Momentum is the "force with which a moving body tends to maintain its velocity and overcome resistance; energy of motion." Once the motion begins, momentum takes over to keep it moving. One action begets another.

If you look at successful people, you'll find they are all action-oriented. They don't wait for things to happen to them; they are always the ones who start—and keep—the momentum going. They don't let inertia set in. Taking action doesn't lead only to success in business. In my book *Diamonds Under Pressure*, I cited a study that was done of approximately forty thousand people in the world who are now over one hundred years old. What they have most in common is not their special diet or their exercise routine. The main trait they all share is that they continue to be engaged in life. They interact with other people, they have hobbies, they work in their gardens, and they take an interest in the world around them. They laugh and they cry often. Instead of bemoaning the fact that they have only a short time left to live, they enjoy every precious moment.

Don't use age as an excuse.

WE have many excuses for not doing things in our lives. One of the most frequent is that we are "too old," especially when it comes to trying something new. Many people believe that as they get older, their brain power will diminish. Not so, according to Dr. Arthur Winter. If we keep using our brains, we limit the deterioration that takes place. "Research is now proving that much of the deterioration in memory and intellectual function we at one time blamed on age is actually due to disuse," says Dr. Winter. "If you don't take action, your brain, like your muscles, may become 'flabby.'"

The "action" Dr. Winter speaks about is both physical and intellectual. When Charles Schultz, creator of the beloved cartoon *Peanuts*, was in his fifties, he felt that he was slowing down. He just didn't "do much" anymore and he wasn't sure what he was still capable of doing. He thought about what he would like to do, and what kept coming up was hockey. He had played hockey as a youngster, and loved the game. But he was over fifty now; he couldn't just join a young men's hockey team. So he created his own team of over-fifty players. It became so popular, he formed a league of over-fifty players. Since he enjoyed it so much, and kept on playing, he kept forming leagues for older and older players. Now Charles Schultz is over seventy, and he belongs to the league of over-seventy hockey teams. And, he says, it is this activity that keeps him feeling younger, more energetic, and able to accomplish more than he did at age fifty.

Surround yourself with energy.

ONE of the reasons Charles Schultz is able to capitalize on his energetic activity is because he is not alone. When he created a hockey team, he found other people who were also looking for ways to become more active and increase their energy levels. All the team members inspire and energize each other.

I find the same principle applies in business. When I first started trying to get a television show, I did not know very much about that industry. I did a lot of research, and met with several people who were able to give me valuable advice about the actions I needed to take. As I went on, I began to gather a team of experts around me, each one specializing in a different area of the industry. Not only did they add value and experience to my presentations, the collective energy we presented to syndicators was impressive. This group energy was what helped me get my show on the air.

They say that two heads are better than one. The same is true for energy. Most of the time, combining two sources of energy makes both entities much more powerful.

There are many sources of energy available to us, if we just seek them out. Find people you admire, and make them part of your inner circle. Remember that mentors come in all shapes and sizes—you can find them in many places. A mentor doesn't have to be rich or famous, or even alive. You can become inspired by the actions of people in history. Go to the library and study biographies of men and women who have achieved greatness in their lives.

Don't be afraid to ask people for help. Most people enjoy being asked and are willing to share whatever and whenever they can. Be specific about what you want. Do you want information about how an industry works? Do you need advice about a particular situation? Are you asking for a job or a recommendation? This makes it easier for people to know whether or not they are able to give you what you need.

Read motivational books and listen to audiotapes. Thousands of inspirational works are available to us. Listen to many different people until you find someone who ignites your passion. Let that person's positive energy become part of your own.

76

Surround yourself with high-energy people.

HAVE you ever attended a high-energy event like a football game or rock concert? If so, then you know that it is almost impossible to keep yourself calm in those surroundings. You can't help but absorb the energy and enthusiasm you feel around you. The same is true when you surround yourself with an inner circle of high-energy, enthusiastic people. They don't have to have frenetic, "jumping around" energy. It's intense, focused energy you're looking for.

Observe these people. See what they do, and how they do it. Emulate their methods. Try doing some of the things that they do. You don't have to do exactly what they do; put your own spin on it. But you will see that many successful people have similar habits and techniques that will probably work for you as well.

Ask five or six people you admire to be your mentors. You may think they are too busy, or you might be afraid to ask. The truth is, most successful people love to be asked. It's a great compliment. You're not asking for their attention twenty-four hours a day. You're asking for permission to call them once in a while when you're facing a challenge or trying to solve a problem and need some advice or suggestions. If they're too busy to help, they'll let you know. Then you can call another one of the mentors you've lined up.

77

Use your physical surroundings as a source of energy.

THERE may come a time when you feel that you are performing below par. Perhaps you've been working too hard for too long without taking a needed break. Or maybe you haven't been sleeping well at night. Whatever the cause, this lack of energy can be frustrating and depressing.

There is, however, an important step you can take to keep those low-energy times to a minimum: create an energy-conducive environment.

- Fill your home and/or office with plants and flowers. You don't have to have a green thumb; if you're a natural born plant killer, buy fresh flowers every few days. Not only does greenery make your environment more pleasant, it also gives off oxygen that can help raise your energy level. If you have a yard or lawn, create an interesting landscape. A few years ago, I moved to a new town. My original goal was to find a place in the mountains, surrounded by deep woods. When it became apparent that this wasn't practical for my lifestyle or my family's needs, I compromised by planting fifty-seven trees around the yard and creating my own suburban woodland. Now I can sit outside every evening and use my quiet time, surrounded by evergreens, to relax and rejuvenate.

- Be aware of lighting. Let in as much sunlight as possible. When that's not possible, make sure the light is appropriate for your needs. If you're in an office, you need light that's bright but not glaring. If you're at home, you might want to install dimmer switches so that you have the ability to turn down the lights when you just want to relax and listen to music.

- Choose a warm color scheme. Mix bright colors with more soothing earth tones.

- Stock up on inspirational reading material. Subscribe to magazines that focus on health, diet, and high achievement. Keep your favorite books within reach so that you can reread stimulating passages whenever your spirit needs a lift.

You are a product of your environment. So choose the environment that will best develop you toward your objective. Analyze your life in terms of its environment. Are the things around you helping you toward success—or are they holding you back?

W. CLEMENT STONE

Action added equals results multiplied.

How many times have you said these words, "I know I should do that, but I just don't have the time"? Take exercising, for instance. Millions of people use the "no time" excuse. Yet once you start exercising on a regular basis, you find that you have much more energy than you used to, and you can do more things in a day. So the half hour or forty-five minutes you find for exercise can actually add several hours to your day. Some actions that you think will pull away from your time actually add to it.

One action does not necessarily produce just one result. In fact, one action often produces multiple results. One hour invested in exercise can give you three or four more hours of energy. One after-hours phone call to reach an important client might give you three or four more other leads or contacts. It's like throwing fuel into a moving train. The train picks up more and more speed as you go along. So that one action you add on is going to help your success train pick up speed and keep moving for a long time to come.

Effective action is 30 percent what you know, and 70 percent how you feel about what you know.

ATTITUDE is everything. Your accomplishments multiply a thousand-fold when you infuse them with energy, excitement, and passion. The other day, someone told me about a woman I would be working with on my television show. He said, "Oh, you'll love her. She's so dynamic and enthusiastic." People never say, "You'll love her. She's so intelligent and has so many degrees." It's not what this woman knows that really impresses people, but how she gets that knowledge across. She's excited about what she knows, about what she's doing and how she can help. And that excitement is truly contagious. Everyone she works with is more productive when she's around. If you have the choice of hiring two people with the same background, the same skills, and the same academic degrees, you will always choose the one with the highest degree—of excitement and enthusiasm. It's what makes the difference, hands down.

I found that I could find the energy . . . that I could find the determination to keep on going. I learned that your mind can amaze your body, if you just keep telling yourself, I can do it . . . I can do it . . . I can do it!

JON ERICKSON

80

Capitalize on your personal energy level.

WHEN I start to write about a subject, I often consult the dictionary to see where the word comes from, and to be sure I understand it completely. When I looked up "energy," I was surprised to find it defined simply as "the capacity to do work." It comes from the Greek word *enérgeia*, meaning activity, which stems from the Greek word *érg*, meaning work. What it boils down to is that the amount of energy you have determines your ability to take action.

People are born with natural energy levels. Some people are born with naturally high energy levels, and some are born with lower levels. Having a higher energy level is good, but is not necessarily an advantage. High energy is not always focused and is often easily distracted. The idea is to recognize your own energy level, work to increase it if it is low, and learn to harness it if it is too high.

There are also many outside factors that influence our energy levels, including health, stressful circumstances, and the weather. If you are not experiencing optimal health, your capacity to do work will diminish. If you are in a stressful situation, your energy may be temporarily raised, but it may also leave you physically and emotionally drained and unable to sustain activity for any length of time.

Some people have more energy in the morning; others have a difficult time getting started, but are raring to go at night. I'm one of those evening people. I'm simply not at my best first thing in the morning; I need time to warm up. So I use that time to focus myself on what I need to accomplish that day. Whenever possible, I schedule appointments for later in the day. I often make phone calls "after hours"—and I reach a lot of people by calling between four and six P.M. And, since I'm on the East Coast, it's a perfect time to make calls to my West Coast clients. I'm often highly energized at ten or eleven at night, and I get some of my best work done at these hours.

Obviously, not everyone is a night person. Joe Bourdow of Val-Pak is definitely a morning person. Fresh out of college, Bourdow began his working career as a morning radio announcer in Staunton, Virginia. Even though he's no longer in radio, the morning work time has remained high energy for him. "To this day, I save the first couple of hours in the morning to accomplish most of my thinking and setting goals for the day," says Bourdow, "before I get involved in meetings or conversations or things that I can't control. That way, I know that I'm going to have a good day by nine in the morning."

Bourdow's trick is to overschedule his morning. "I get three hours' worth of work done in the first two hours," he says. "I get up such a head of steam that by the time everybody else shows up here at headquarters, I'm fully engaged and usually have a good deal of energy throughout the day."

That's a prime example of taking action. Bourdow doesn't have to get to his office before everyone else, but he knows that's his peak energy time. You can find your own peak energy time as well. For the next two weeks, observe your own working patterns. Don't change your routine, just record your personal peaks and valleys. Do you work best in the morning, afternoon, or evening? Keep a chart of your energy highs and lows. After two weeks, you will come up with a recognizable energy pattern.

Now review your working habits. See what you can do to change your daily routine so that the times you need to be most productive coincide with your peak energy hours. You'll be amazed at how much more you can get done.

81

Exercise for energy.

WITH our busy twenty-first-century lives, it's hard to find the time to exercise. We often feel that with all we have to do, we have no energy left for exercise. But research has shown that exercise can actually increase your feelings of energy. In fact, it can restore your energy so that you have enough to get all your daily tasks accomplished and still have some left over to enjoy life.

Scientists are not exactly sure why exercise makes us feel better, but it does. One theory is that exercise increases our brain's production of hormones called endorphins. Endorphins have been shown to affect those areas of the brain associated with emotion and behavior and to help elevate mood and decrease feelings of fatigue. This has sometimes been described as a "runner's high." Another theory says that exercise increases the amount of neurotransmitter activity in the brain. These are chemicals that are also believed to regulate mood and emotions. And a third theory says that it is simply the fact that exercise increases the amount of oxygen that is transported to the brain that gives us those elevated feelings. Whatever the cause, the result is the same. Exercise increases our feelings of health, well-being and self-esteem, and energy.

And there's even more good news. A 1994 study by Dr. Robert Thayer reported in the *Journal of Personality and Social Psychology* that the primary effect of moderate exercise (in this case a ten-minute brisk walk) was energy enhancement. Another study conducted at Cornell University showed that even small amounts of exercise have positive physical and psychological effects. So several short (ten-minute) exercise breaks during the day can have the same effect as one forty-minute workout.

Regular exercise can make a big difference in your overall energy levels and in how you feel about yourself. This is something Joe Bourdow recently discovered. Not too long ago he was driving home after work and passed a sign advertising the services of a personal trainer. "I thought, 'Should I? Can I?'" says Bourdow. "I hadn't exercised since I was cut from the baseball team at T. C. Williams High School in 1968." Intimidated by the thought of starting an exercise program, Bourdow nonetheless decided to talk to the trainer, who then put him on a program of forty-five minutes of exercise three days a week.

"I found a trainer who knows how to take care of the body of a middle-aged, not particularly in-shape person. And it's made a tremendous difference in terms of energy and health," adds Bourdow. "And, if you've had a bad day and you're frustrated about work, you just stop by the gym, hit the punching bag, and think about all those people who annoyed you so much. After about half an hour, you forget what you were so mad about. It's certainly a reasonable investment for what you get back."

82

Improve your food-to-energy ratio.

NOT all energy patterns are inborn. Some are habits—good and bad—that we have learned. And those habits are often based on diet and exercise. I'm not going to recommend any particular diet or exercise plan for you. You are a unique individual and must discover for yourself what foods and activities are healthiest for you. However, I will talk about some basic biological facts that can and do affect your energy production.

First, it's important to realize that we are, in truth, what we eat. Food is the fuel that makes our bodies go. Think of your body as an expensive automobile. If you fill the car with low-grade gasoline, it will run for a while but it will not reach peak performance. If you drive it around long enough without filling the gas tank, it won't go any farther. And if you don't give it periodic tune-ups, it will run less and less efficiently until it breaks down all together.

Our bodies are the same. Common sense tells you that your body needs lean protein, fruits, vegetables, and lots of water. If your only fuel is junk food, sweets, and carbohydrates, you will function for short periods of time, but you will soon run out of steam. Using artificial stimulants like caffeine and sugary treats (especially cakes, cookies, and candies) for a quick "energy fix" only gives you a short-lived burst, after which you crash and burn. Some carbohydrates have been touted as high-energy foods, but, according to Anne Louise Gittleman in her book *Your Body Knows Best*, "the most commonly consumed carbohydrates (like pasta, bread, bagels and potatoes) actually quickly release sugar into the bloodstream and then—if not immediately used—this sugar is turned into body fat." So the sugar you're using for a burst of energy is most likely to end up slowing you down with extra weight. Food is a powerful drug, and should be treated as such. If you choose healthy foods, you automatically increase your body's fuel-burning efficiency. Consult your doctor or nutritionist to set up a food plan that will help you enjoy a healthy, energetic lifestyle.

83

Rest to gather strength, no more.

Have you ever slept longer than you should have, only to find when you wake up that you're actually overtired? It happens all the time. Our bodies need rest. But we are not designed for too much rest either. The purpose of rest is to gather strength for life.

There are people who spend their whole lives waiting to retire. They dream about having all the time in the world to sleep late, sit on the beach, play some golf. Then when it happens, they go stir-crazy. Every animal in nature rests for survival, so that later it can hunt for food, escape predators, protect its young, and construct its shelters. We are built the same way. But because of our superior brains, we have devised ways that make it easier to survive. We can get into lazy habits that allow us to rest unnecessarily.

We sleep long hours. We watch television for five or six hours at a time and think we're relaxing. There's nothing wrong with taking a twenty-minute power nap during the day if you're tired. It can be a great pleasure to sit down and watch a television show you've been looking forward to seeing. But rest is not an end unto itself. It should be used for refueling and rejuvenation, to give you the energy you need to actively participate in life.

84

Redefine your concept of "vacation."

I can't go away for longer than three days. After that, my head is clear, I've got my energy back, and I can't wait to get back to work. In fact, I'd rather go on a three-day getaway than take the standard one- or two-week vacation that fits the usual definition of the word.

That's just me. If you love to travel, there's nothing wrong with taking an extended vacation to be able to explore and sightsee. But don't think that every vacation has to be packed full of things to do. Sometimes the best break can be a weekend puttering in the yard or going to a museum in your hometown. What you want to do is choose the activity (or lack of it) that relaxes you, that lets you leave pressures and deadlines aside and enjoy doing something that gives you pure pleasure, and that reenergizes you for the work week ahead.

Some people spend the entire year dreaming of their vacation. Then when it finally comes, they're under an incredible amount of pressure to have a good time every minute. They come back to work with more tension than when they left. If you are spending all of your work life just waiting for vacation, you may be in the wrong job. The goal of life is to find both work and nonwork pleasurable, to look forward to going to work just as much as you look forward to going on vacation.

85

Recreation = re-creation.

THE movie *Searching for Bobby Fischer* is about a young chess champion who learns at a very early age what pressure can do to undermine productivity and self-esteem. The young boy, winning tournament after tournament, suddenly began to lose—and to lose his confidence. There were those around him who wanted him to keep playing and practicing over and over again until he won again. But his father, seeing what the intense stress was doing to his son, took him away on a week-long fishing trip.

They didn't play chess, talk about chess, or think about chess. They fished. And when they came back, the boy won again.

Sometimes there is no better way to improve the quality of our actions than by stopping them altogether. When we are intensively active for a long period of time (and the length of the period varies from individual to individual), our brain gets overheated. We come to a point where we may be going through the motions, but we are not thinking clearly or productively. That's when we need to rest, relax, and rejuvenate.

Rest comes in many forms. For some people, it's a good night's sleep, or even a "power nap" in the middle of the day. Studies have shown that napping for about twenty minutes gives us the rest we need without making us over-tired. For some people, the best way to rejuvenate is to stop working, exercise for an hour or so, and come back to work again. For me, it can be taking a bike ride with my children in the middle of the day, or playing the violin for fifteen or twenty minutes between phone calls. One friend of mine takes a break by making phone calls to raise funds for his favorite charity. While that may not seem like rest to most of us, it's a break in his usual routine and leaves him with positive energy to return to his daily chores. Whatever type of break you take, when you come back to work again, you will feel calmer and more capable. You'll be ready to begin again with renewed energy and a fresh attitude.

SUMMARY

- Energy determines how we move forward physically, mentally and emotionally. We can learn to harness our untapped reservoirs of energy to keep us motivated and inspired. This not only allows us to take more actions, but to make those actions more powerful and vibrant.

- Energy is governed by the laws of physics. When you "have no energy," you are experiencing inertia—matter stays at rest until it is acted upon by an outside force. That outside force is an action you take. Then when you take an action, you start building momentum, which keeps the energy flowing.

- Getting older is not an excuse for doing less. Studies have long shown that people who retire and do little to fill their time are very soon dissatisfied with their lives of leisure. Many of the illnesses and depression associated with old age have shown marked improvement when activity and exercise were prescribed and followed.

- Surround yourself with energy. Find people with knowledge and experience to share; use their energy to increase your own.

- You are a product of your environment—so design your space in a way that keeps you motivated and inspired. Are the things around you helping you toward success—or are they holding you back? Surround yourself with images that stimulate energy production and positive thought.

- Action added = results multiplied. One action does not necessarily produce just one result. In fact, there is no way of knowing beforehand just what results your one action will set in motion. Like throwing fuel into a moving train, adding action keeps you going stronger and longer than you could ever foresee.

- Energy and enthusiasm are contagious. It's very hard to get people on your side when you're lethargic and dispassionate. On the other hand, people will want to be part of your team when you exhibit passion for your ideas. Your attitude always determines your altitude.

- High energy does not mean constant work. Everyone needs a break once in a while, time to regroup and recuperate. Do whatever relaxes you most. That may mean sitting and reading a book for an hour, playing a strenuous game of tennis, or going out for dinner with friends. Even a twenty-minute break from work can serve as the rest your brain and body need to reenergize.

ACTION PLANS

- When you feel that you are low on energy, take one action that you don't feel like doing. Make one more phone call. Do fifteen minutes of exercise. Run an errand for someone in need. Then check your energy level again—you'll be surprised to find you have more energy than when you were sitting around feeling tired and blue.

- Search out as many sources of energy as you can:

  ⇒ Ask people for help. Mentors are not difficult to find—most people are flattered to be asked and more than willing to share advice and information.

  ⇒ Read biographies and become inspired by the actions of historical figures who achieved greatness in their lives.

  ⇒ Read motivational books and listen to audiotapes until you find someone who ignites your energy, then let that person's energy become part of your own.

- Discover your personal energy peak time:

  ⇒ For two weeks, observe and record your normal work patterns.

  ⇒ Chart your time of highest and lowest energy.

  ⇒ Review your work habits and adjust your routine so that your most energy-consuming tasks fall into your hours of highest energy.

- Review your diet and exercise routines. Are you eating balanced, healthy meals? If not, consult a doctor or nutritionist to help you choose foods that are best for your personal needs. Join a gym, hire a personal trainer, or simply get out and walk. You cannot function at your most productive level if your body is run-down and out of shape.

ACTION STEPS FOR MARKETING YOURSELF

O NE day last summer my six-year-old daughter, Hallie, was helping me wash my car. I was planning to sell it and wanted it to look its very best. She loves to paint and draw, so she helped me make a large "For Sale" sign to place in the window. We got the car all clean and shiny and I parked it at the end of the driveway so passersby might see it and the sign. I gathered the sponges and pails we had been using and headed back toward the garage.

All of a sudden I heard Hallie, in her loudest six-year-old voice, shouting "Car for sale! My daddy's car for sale!" I came out of the garage and said, "Hallie, what are you doing?"

"Daddy," she said, "nobody's going to know the car is for sale if we don't tell them!"

It seems Hallie had a natural understanding of the power of marketing. Even though we're not all salespeople, we're all selling something. It may be a product, a service, or an idea, but we're selling something. And in order to sell, we've got to get the word out. Even Dr. Fred Epstein, renowned neurosurgeon, has his own public relations agent. Many people are shocked at that; they don't think a doctor should be doing PR. But suppose a family in Alaska or Oklahoma has a child with a spinal cord tumor they've been told is inoperable. They don't know where to turn. Then one day, they open a magazine and read about the incredible results Dr. Epstein is having with patients just like their child. They take the child to see Dr. Epstein and he is able to save that child's life. All because of a little publicity.

Your own situation is probably not that dramatic. But there is no reason to be ashamed or embarrassed to market yourself. Never be afraid to stand at the end of your driveway and shout your message to anyone who will listen.

86

Promote yourself and your successes.

UNLESS you are rich and famous and have hired a public relations firm to get your name in print, you must promote yourself everywhere you go. Most of us are not used to thinking that way. We've been taught to be modest, and not to blow our own horns. But you want to be sure that people know the value of what you have to offer, and the only way to do that is by spreading the word.

Of course, promoting is easiest when you have a strong belief in the product or service you're selling, the cause you're advancing, the job you're performing. If you don't believe what you have has value, you're not going to be comfortable spreading the word.

You spread the word by communicating with people, by sharing information that might be helpful to them, by creating value for them. Marc Roberts, one of the most successful sports agents in the country, is a client and a close friend of mine. No one is better at promotion than he is. He once gave me this example of promotion. Suppose you were selling refrigerators, for example. You started out with 1,500; you've sold 500 and you have 1,000 left. You would promote the fact that you've already sold 500 refrigerators, not that you've got 1,000 left in the warehouse and the overhead is eating into your profits.

You can promote yourself by promoting others as well. Recently, I read *Turned On* by the Marriott's Roger Dow. Roger is a friend and a mentor to me. I bought several copies of the book and had him autograph them. I then sent the book to people I was currently working with, people I was hoping to work with, and longtime clients. I included a note that said, "I thought you might enjoy this from my friend Roger." Although it might seem that I was promoting Roger's book by doing this, I was really promoting myself as well by creating value for my prospects and clients. It showed that I was thinking of them.

Create a list of people to whom you will send periodic notices of your own accomplishments, articles that might be of interest to them, events they might want to attend. If you get one deal or business connection out of this kind of promotion, it will more than pay for the cost of the mailing. Promoting yourself in this way can help keep you motivated as well. When you're in the middle of sending out letters, licking envelopes, faxing, and e-mailing, it gets you excited about how you're moving your business forward. You're creating a network of supporters who can help build your business for you.

Tell everyone about your goals.

MANY things do not seem real to us until we speak of them out loud. It's one thing to have a dream you keep to yourself; if you don't make it come true, no one but you will know about it. Those dreams are usually the ones that fade away with time.

If you're really serious about reaching a goal, talk about it. Tell everyone. Get feedback. Some people will discourage you, but others will contribute valuable advice. The simple act of pushing a dream out of your mind and into the real world helps it take on a tangible shape. Once you tell other people about your goals, you make a commitment to them. It's almost a challenge—now you've got to come through.

The world has the habit of making room for the man whose words and actions show that he knows where he is going

NAPOLEON HILL

Discover your uniqueness and differentiate yourself.

Pianist Arthur Schnabel once said, "The notes I handle no better than many pianists. But the pauses between the notes—ah, that is where the art resides!" It's not what you do, it's how you do it that counts. A note on a piano is a note on a piano, no matter what you do. What makes you an artist is your own interpretation, your own rhythm, the timing and pauses you put in between the notes.

Whether you're a painter, a salesman, a mother, a boxer, a writer, a construction worker—whatever your profession, what makes you unique is what you bring to the table. Nobody else can duplicate that. That's what you must let people know about what you do. That differentiating factor is what you sell; it's your special value. No one else can bring your particular knowledge or your life experiences to a project. You are more than a commodity; you have yourself to share. And if you don't share your unique qualities, you are selling yourself—and everyone else you are dealing with—short.

There can be no great courage where there is no confidence or assurance, and half the battle is in the conviction that we can do what we undertake.

Orison Swett Marden

89

Never say bad things about people. If someone else is saying bad things about people, stop them.

THE first part is not that difficult; the second part is. You may be tempted to badmouth people, especially if they are your competitors. But that never helps your cause, it only weakens your position. Sometimes, other people put down your competition to see how you'll react. Your answer should always be, "I've heard good things about them" or "I really don't know about that." Then go on to talk about your strengths rather than their weaknesses.

Never put yourself in the position where people have bad things to say about you. People you deal with should always have positive perceptions of you. Always treat them fairly, and do more than is expected. Build up your own value by proving that you are trustworthy and that you will go out of your way to provide value for others. That way, if someone (your competition, perhaps) should say something bad about you, you've got your excellent reputation as your defense.

90

Communicate using all available media.

IT'S not always necessary to interrupt someone's busy schedule with a personal phone call. Sometimes you just want to leave a message—or an impression. Voice-mail can be an effective method. Call someone late at night or early in the morning when you know they won't be there. Then you can leave a message saying, "Just wanted to let you know there's a TV program scheduled for tonight about that new technology we discussed." Or, "Here's a company that can use your services."

Use e-mail. Busy executives who never have time to return phone calls check their e-mail often and are more likely to respond electronically. It's often a good way to make initial contact and assess a person's interest in what you have to offer. This can be especially effective when you've been referred to someone in a large company or organization. You can send the person an e-mail, letting them know you were referred to them (and by whom), and that they will be receiving a packet of your materials. Then you send them the information and follow it up with another e-mail asking when a convenient time to call them might be. You'll often find the people respect the e-mail more than they do a cold call.

And don't forget about "snail mail"—what techies call those letters delivered the old-fashioned way, via the U.S. Postal Service. It's amazing what a difference a personalized card or letter can make. Randy Rosler, president and founder of Introknocks Corp., has developed a line of greeting cards designed to increase the effectiveness of business communications.

"Only 4 percent of all direct mail is handwritten," says Rosler. "With that in mind, think about how your correspondence will stand out when it arrives in a colored envelope, handwritten, with a first-class stamp." You can send cards to contacts just to say "hi" and keep in touch, to prospective clients (and perhaps include an article on their industry), or a note of appreciation to a client, customer, or colleague.

Rosler's cards are lighthearted and creative. For instance, one shows a man and a woman trying to squeeze into a crowded elevator. The inside of the card reads: *I realize you keep a busy schedule, but is it possible you could squeeze me in?* Rosler suggests you then add a personal message inside, like: "I have a great idea that can benefit your business. Let's meet so I can share it with you."

Another card shows the inner workings of a clock on the outside with the phrase: *Time—Your most valuable commodity.* Inside, it says: *Thanks for sharing some with me.* It has a perforated slot to insert your business card, and plenty of room to write your own message. It's a perfect message for someone who has given a sales lead over the phone, someone who has helped you with your business, or anyone who has given up some of their time to give you a hand.

Another card in Rosler's line shows a picture of a globe with a red ribbon wrapped around it. It says: *Referrals from you mean the world to me.* On the inside the card simply reads: *Thank you.* Obviously, this is a card you would send to someone who has referred you to someone else. It may be a simple message, but it's one a lot of people neglect to give. By sending a simple thank-you, you're separating yourself from the crowd (not many people send thank-you's). It's the type of gesture people appreciate and remember. Whether you use a preprinted card like Rosler's, or a blank card with your own message written in, your goal is to leave a positive and personal impression.

SUMMARY

- Since we are all salespeople of one kind or another, we must all learn to market ourselves. There is never a reason to be ashamed or embarrassed to do a little self-promotion.

- Spread the word about yourself, your product or your service by communicating with people, by sharing information that might be helpful to them, and by creating value for them.

- Capitalize on your own strengths and differences to sell yourself. If all products were alike, everyone would use the same one. We buy a product because it has some unique property that we need or enjoy. The same goes for people. We "buy" what they have to sell because of their unique qualities. Find out what makes you unique, what you bring to the table (based on your knowledge and experience) that gives you special value.

- Build up your own value by proving yourself competent and trustworthy, not by demeaning the competition. When you say bad things about others, you only reflect badly on yourself.

ACTION PLANS

- Create a list of people to whom you can promote yourself. Send them:

  ⇒ periodic notices of your own accomplishments
  ⇒ articles that might be of interest to them
  ⇒ events they might want to attend
  ⇒ birthday cards
  ⇒ notes of congratulations on a move or promotion

- Tell everyone about your goals. Goals are more likely to become reality if you talk about them. Get feedback. Perhaps the people you talk to can give you advice as to how to proceed.

- Try using different methods to contact hard-to-reach individuals:

  ⇒ voice-mail—leave a message that doesn't require a call-back
  ⇒ e-mail—busy people are often more likely to respond to an e-mail than to a phone message
  ⇒ snail mail—a personalized card or letter can stand out and be an effective attention-getter

NOTES

ACTION STEPS FOR OVERCOMING OBSTACLES

INTO every life a little rain must fall. Some lives are flooded with adversity, others have sprinkles of it here and there. But everyone goes through it. The purpose of this section is to help you understand that obstacles that push us back when we're trying to go forward are not only testing us. They're also giving us an opportunity to learn great lessons. Challenges present us with the greatest opportunities. How you deal with adversity depends on how you view it, how you react, how you move in the face of rejection and failure.

If you're taking actions that present no challenges, you're not going after anything important. Everything worth having involves some sort of risk. If you want to achieve something big, you're going to run into obstacles that are just as large. These action steps can help you face those challenges and come out wiser, stronger, and happier.

91

Concentrate on what you *can* do, not on what you *can't* do.

ONE of the most important traits of highly successful people is that they are optimists. They don't waste their energy on their own fears and negative attitudes. That doesn't mean they walk around humming happy tunes all the time. It does mean they take a generally constructive attitude toward life. According to Brian Tracy, optimists have three basic qualities in common:

1. Optimists look for the good in every person and in every situation.

2. Optimists find the valuable lessons in a setback or reversal.

3. Optimists are solution-oriented rather than problem-oriented.

When optimists meet someone, they note his good qualities first before they see any flaws. They expect each experience to be a positive one. They look for the good in every situation and look for ways to capitalize on it.

If, however, a situation should turn out to be negative, or to have negative aspects, they don't give up and walk away. They learn from the failure or setback, and use what they have learned to do better the next time. If you study the histories of most successful people, you will find that they did not become successful until after they had suffered a major loss or failure.

But it is the third aspect of optimism that is the most important. In fact, your ability to solve problems effectively determines everything that happens to you in life. And the better you are at solving problems, the more complicated problems you get to solve.

Optimists are future-oriented. When a problem arises, optimists say, "How can I solve this? What's the next step I can take?" Pessimists are past-oriented. When a problem arises, they say, "How could this happen to me?

Whose fault is this? Who can I blame? How can I cover this up?" The optimist does not waste time with these questions, but faces the problem head-on and takes immediate action to solve the problem.

Don't be concerned if you have negative thoughts when problems appear. Everyone does. The real trouble begins when you can't get beyond these thoughts. But here's the amazing truth about optimism and problem-solving: As soon as you start looking for solutions, you become an optimist! Picture this: You're on a country lane and you come to a fork in the road. You don't know which way to go. You come to a stop, start crying, and become convinced that you will never reach your destination. You are now a pessimist.

A few minutes later, you get tired of crying. You move toward the fork on the right. You realize that by making this decision you'll either reach your destination or find out that you have to come back to this point and take the fork on the left. Either way, you've solved the immediate problem—and you've become an instant optimist! Which proves you can go from pessimism to optimism in a matter of minutes, simply by switching your concentration away from the problem and onto the solution.

Both optimism and pessimism are catching. It's important to be careful what you're passing on to someone else. Roger Dow of the Marriott tells how he learned this lesson. Dow was a college wrestler. As a freshman he entered a tournament where he drew as his opponent a returning national champion. He was terrified. Seconds before the match, his coach pulled him aside.

"Roger," said the coach, "you've got the whole season in front of you. Don't get hurt."

Dow lost the match, 20-3. "To this day I wonder if it would have been any closer if the coach had pulled me aside and said, 'Roger, I understand that since this guy won the national championship he skips practice three times a week. He's not expecting anyone to beat him. Go out there and surprise him.' Would I have won the match? I don't know. Would the score have been closer? You betcha."

That coach had no idea his words would be remembered so many years later. It took the optimist in Roger Dow to learn a lesson from his bitter defeat. He learned a lesson and kept moving forward. It is not the defeat that's important, it's the action that follows.

The boy who is going to make a great man . . . must not make up his mind merely to overcome a thousand obstacles, but to win in spite of a thousand repulses and defeats.

THEODORE ROOSEVELT

92

Don't let illusion cloud your perception.

WILLIAM Blake once said, "If the doors of perception were cleansed everything would appear to man as it is, infinite." Most of the barriers that we come across in life are illusions. We are stopped by the words and thoughts of others. "You can't do that." "No one has ever done that before." "You can't get there from here." We're stopped by these barriers that have no walls, no railings, no barricades, no blockades, no perimeters. The only true barrier is our own perception.

The only thing that can break through that perception is action. When the doors of perception are cleansed, when the illusions are washed away, limitless possibilities come into view. You can get there from here. You might have to take a route other than the one you had originally planned on taking. You might have to take a risk, perhaps fall on your face a few times. But the further you go, the fewer barriers you encounter. And the only way to discover this truth is to make the journey yourself.

We must look for the opportunity in every difficulty instead of being paralyzed at the thought of the difficulty in every opportunity.

WALTER E. COLE

93

Challenge yourself every day.

I<small>F</small> we keep our dreams only in our minds, they remain vague and have a "someday" quality about them. When we write them down, it's almost as if we tell ourselves, "Okay. Now you've made a commitment. I dare you to follow through on it."

It's possible to let dreams go by, but it's difficult to ignore a challenge. Think about times when someone dared you to do something. It probably spurred you on, got your blood pumping, and gave your brain a jump-start. A challenge creates energy, and energy enables us to take action. Challenges get us thinking of ways to go beyond our present limitations (real or imagined). When we're heading into the unknown, our adrenaline starts flowing. We get "hungrier." We become more focused. The stakes become higher.

When you challenge yourself to achieve specific goals, you pull yourself forward. You may not make it every time. There are times when you will experience setbacks and failures. But that only makes the challenge greater; you are being given an opportunity to begin again and perhaps find a better route. Every challenge is a learning experience. You don't learn from the things you already know how to do. You learn from striving, stretching, reaching, and traveling roads you have not gone down before.

Children know this instinctively. Children face challenges every day; they start off knowing nothing, so everything is a challenge to them. Kids have an insatiable curiosity—they are seldom afraid to try new things. And the joy they experience when they have mastered even the smallest skill is immediately apparent. There is nothing sweeter than the sound of a child's exuberant laughter when he first learns to take a few steps, to catch a ball, or to say a new word. We must learn to recapture this joy in small accomplishments. You don't have to wait until you reach your goal to be proud of yourself. Pat yourself on the back for writing two pages of your novel today. Feel good about staying one half hour later at work to make more phone calls. Enjoy the fact that you went to the library and researched job possibilities.

Feel good about your accomplishments—then move on. If you wrote two pages today, write three pages tomorrow. If you've stayed one half hour later to make calls, try staying one hour later the next time. After you've researched job possibilities, send out your resume or make some networking phone calls. Use the pride and energy you get from each small accomplishment to fuel the next steps forward.

94

Find problems to solve that others run away from.

PEOPLE who always look for the easy way out don't reap the big rewards. Those who are willing to step in when others say the road is too difficult are those who truly succeed. A friend of mine was doing fairly well as a sales representative for an insurance company. Then he was moved to another state. He left behind all his old leads and contacts. He knew it could take a long time to build up his clientele in the new territory. So he decided to take on all the complainers and problem customers he could find. The other sales reps were happy to unload their difficult clients, those who were constantly dissatisfied or were not paying their premiums.

My friend sat down with these customers and listened to their problems and complaints. He found ways to solve them. He helped these customers with their insurance needs and, as a result, he helped himself get ahead. He took on the customers no one else wanted, and he soon became the number-one insurance sales rep in the country. He did not run away from problems; he embraced them instead. He saw problems not as obstacles, but as opportunities for growth.

95

If you come to a barrier you can't pass through—re-create yourself.

SOME barriers are impenetrable. If you keep trying the same old way to get by them, you will inevitably fail. So you must find new ways. Create something new. Discover new passages. You must adapt to the situation in which you find yourself. If you keep hitting your head against the wall trying to get a project done, it may be that you need to change your direction and go around the wall instead.

Here's an example. If I'm trying to get business from a company I've never worked with before, I always call on the person at the top—the owner, the president, the CEO. Sometimes I get through, but other times I get nowhere. I could give up on that company. Instead, I contact someone in another area of the company, perhaps a top distributor for that organization, and make myself known to him or her. That person can then refer me back to the top brass. If I find that I have reached a dead end, I take what I have learned from this experience and move on.

It is the scientific approach to life. Scientists are faced with a particular problem and search for ways to solve it. When they are trying to discover a new drug, they don't expect to come up with the answer on their first try. They try many different avenues. They know that they will take three steps forward and two steps back, that they will come upon many detours along the way. But they keep re-creating the drug until they find the right combination of chemicals. And, as they're experimenting, they take notice of ways that their findings can be applied in other areas as well. A drug that is being designed to ease arthritis pain, for instance, may be found to have properties that reduce the pain of migraine headaches.

There are three approaches to dealing with the barriers you face. When you come upon a brick wall, you can try to pass it in these ways:

1. *Climb it.* Look for toeholds. Build a ladder. Ask to stand on someone else's shoulders.

2. *Go around it.* Keep moving until you come to the end and travel around the wall. Or find another entry, a tunnel, or a bridge that will get you to the same destination via a different route.

3. *Go through it.* At least make the attempt. You might find out that the wall is only a facade, an illusion that you have constructed out of fear. If it's not a facade, you might not be able to penetrate the wall. But during the attempt you will discover what the wall is made of, how thick and tall it is, and what has happened to others who have tried to climb it. Then the next time you come upon this wall (or one like it), you'll have a head start at getting through. And last but not least, someone on the other side may see your struggle and decide to give you a hand.

So as you come up against a barrier in your life, look for every possible way to climb it, get around it, or go through it. Adapt, adjust, and re-create, adapt, adjust, and re-create again, and eventually you'll come out stronger and wiser on the other side.

96

Don't forget your past rejections.

DWELLING on the past does nothing but slow you down. Learning from it, however, can spur you forward. If you were rejected, ask yourself why. Is there anything you can use to make your next attempt more successful? Even if you feel you were wrongly rejected (and don't we all?), use your anger constructively. An incredible amount of energy goes into anger, and you can choose the way that energy gets utilized. It can eat away at your confidence, willpower, and determination. It can tempt you to take revenge against those who wronged you. Or you can turn it into a positive force that propels you forward and keeps you going past all obstacles.

When you succeed after everyone has said you would fail, that is the best revenge. It's revenge without hurting anyone. If you let those people stop you or bring you down, then they win. If you succeed despite them, then you win. So don't dwell on your rejections, but don't forget about them either. Use them to push you on to new heights.

———

I do not fear failure. I only fear the "slowing up" of the engine inside of me which is pounding, saying, "Keep going, someone must be on top, why not you?"

GEORGE S. PATTON

97

Get mad and get moving.

SOME things are difficult to teach. Some things you just have to learn for yourself. This is one of them: Rejection and failure are just a part of the game. It happens to everyone, and you can let it bring you down and stop you dead, or you can let it energize you to move to even greater heights.

When somebody puts you down, don't believe them! Get mad and get moving. They don't know who you are. They don't know what you're capable of doing. They have no power over you. You have the power to prove them right or prove them wrong. If you want to prove them right, do nothing. Give up your dreams. Stop what you're doing. Feel sorry for yourself.

But if you want to prove them wrong, keep moving. Take action. Use that rejection as fuel to keep you motivated. Just understand that life is never a smooth ride that comes with constant encouragement and approval. It is a bumpy road we travel, and all along the way there are people putting up roadblocks and detours. That doesn't mean you turn around and go home.

Let negative situations energize you instead of pulling you down. There will always be people who tell you that your dreams are impossible. They try to convince you that you don't have the ability or the talent to reach your goals. They say, "That's not the way things are done." They say, "What you're trying to accomplish is so difficult, you might as well give up now."

You can believe those people—or you can turn that negative energy into the driving force that pushes you forward. Create a vision of those naysayers in your mind, and then use that vision as a springboard to prove them wrong. Challenge yourself to show them what you really can do.

Alan Schonberg, founder and chairman of Management Recruiters International, has to deal with rejection all the time—both for himself and for clients he's trying to place. "Rejection is hard for everyone," he says, "but the first thing I always consider is who is rejecting me? What basis do they have to reject me? Are they right? If they're right, I'd better make some changes. And if they're wrong, it's their mistake and their loss."

98

Disabilities early in life are often advantages later on.

Dr. Fred Epstein is a world-renowned pediatric neurosurgeon currently practicing at Beth Israel Medical Center in New York City. He has been praised and hailed as a hero by patients, their parents, and the medical community for developing techniques to operate on brain stem and spinal cord tumors that were previously thought to be fatal for the children who suffered from them. As a child, Fred Epstein was learning disabled.

He was terrible in math and had trouble concentrating. "I probably had attention deficit disorder," he says, "although they didn't have a name for it then. All I knew was that people got mad at me all the time, and I always felt stupid. But in the end, the fact that I've been able to succeed is an illustration that anyone else can too."

Dr. Epstein feels that people with learning disabilities are "wired differently" and may need special help to get over some hurdles. But he also believes that they can learn to compensate for those disabilities and, in fact, become highly motivated, successful adults.

"Those who overcome learning disabilities," says Dr. Epstein, "will outstrip their peers in terms of what they accomplish." That's because "normal" people often hesitate to take chances because they're afraid of looking foolish, afraid of failure. But people with learning disabilities have had lots of experience looking foolish. They've been embarrassed all their lives and they know they have to work hard to get past that. They are usually willing to take the risk of failure because they've been through it so many times before.

So whenever you are tempted to shy away from an opportunity due to fear of failure or embarrassment, think of those who've had to deal with it all their lives, and how little difference it has made in terms of what they have accomplished.

99

Eliminate the "option" of failure.

WHEN the NASA ground crew admitted that failure to return the Apollo 13 crew to Earth was "not an option," they eliminated it as a possibility. They committed themselves so totally to that statement that they were able to focus solely on what they could accomplish.

When you make this kind of commitment, you stop your brain from accepting excuses. Without this commitment, you will waver. You will say the things we all tell ourselves when things get tough: "I'm not sure I can do this," or "I could try this but what's the point? It will never work." If failure is not an option, you will try all kinds of things in the pursuit of success, because you have no choice but to press forward.

100

Life is too serious to be taken seriously.

WHEN stress is at its worst, when the tension is unbearable, when things are looking bleak—it's time to lighten up. The curative powers of humor are incredible. Sometimes humor allows you to fly past it all and to put things in perspective. It's good to laugh at yourself, and to make others laugh as well. Take time for levity. If you hear a good joke pass it on. It's a great way to network. Take a short break during the day and call someone who can use some cheering up. Or send an e-mail. That way, you won't interrupt someone's busy schedule, but you can still brighten his or her day.

Laughter is not only good for health; it usually lets you see things in a different light. Why are comedians funny? It's not that they see different things than we do, it's that they see the same things differently. Listen to your favorite comedians and take a hint from the way they look at life. The best of them take the simple things we do every day in life, the flaws and foibles that make us human, and make us laugh at the absurdity of it all.

But we don't always need comedians to make us laugh at life. We must learn to laugh at ourselves, and to count our blessings. Humor can help you deal with even the most serious of situations. When you look at others who are in truly dire straits, it helps to put your own worries in perspective.

Studies have shown that children laugh anywhere from one hundred to four hundred times a day. The average adult laughs about four times a day. That's sad. Laughter is the best stress-reliever known to man. It opens our creative minds. People want to be around other people who are happy and laughing.

A salesperson I know recently told me the secret of his success—he's a happy person. He admitted that he doesn't have the greatest sales techniques in the world, he's simply upbeat. "That's what gets me in the door and gets me a lot of business," he said. "If people are in a bad mood, I try to turn them around, to make them feel better. I try to lighten up their day. Once I do that, everything else follows. I don't make every sale, but people remember me and welcome me back again."

The reason angels can fly is that they take themselves so lightly.

G. K. CHESTERTON

101

Keep in touch.

ONE of the greatest rewards I have in life is hearing from people who benefit from what I do. I want to hear from you. I want to hear how particular action steps work for you, how you use them, and what you accomplish. Perhaps you have some of your own you might want to share.

You can write to me at:

Farber Training Systems
66 East Sherbrooke Parkway
Livingston, New Jersey 07039

You can call me at (973) 535-9400, or fax me at (973) 535-9466. Or, you can e-mail me at www.barryfarber.com

Let me hear from you!

SUMMARY

- Challenges present us with the greatest opportunities. Everything worth having involves some sort of risk. How you deal with risk and challenge depends on how you react to them. Remember that challenges give us the opportunity to learn great lessons.

- Most highly successful people are true optimists and have three basic qualities in common:

  ⇒ They look for the good in every person and every situation.

  ⇒ They find the valuable lessons in setbacks or reversals.

  ⇒ They are solution-oriented rather than problem-oriented.

- Don't let other people's opinions or illusions stop your progress. They may think what you're trying to do is impossible. They may not be able to do it, but that doesn't mean you can't achieve your goals. Look for the opportunity in every difficulty instead of the difficulty in every opportunity.

- Take the scientific approach to life: know that you may have to conduct many different experiments before you come up with an answer. You may have to adjust and readjust your thinking several times before you reach your goal. But know also that every attempt gives you more information and gets you closer to your ultimate destination.

- Don't dwell on your rejections, but don't forget them either. Use the energy that comes from anger to spur you on and motivate you to succeed despite what others have said or done.

- Make a commitment to success. Eliminate the choice of failure. If failure is not an option, you have no choice but to keep going forward toward success.

- Learn to lighten up. Laughter really is the best medicine, and when you're feeling pressured and overwhelmed, there's nothing like a good joke to brighten your day. Humor also frees up your creative juices, and gets you looking at life in a different light. It's the best stress-reliever known to man.

ACTION PLANS

- When you are faced with a problem or obstacle, become future-oriented. Instead of asking, "Why did this happen to me? Who is to blame for it?" ask yourself, "How can I solve this? What is the next step I can take?"

- Challenge yourself every day; make yourself do something new and unusual. Don't just tell yourself to do it—phrase it in terms of a dare: "I dare you to network with three new people today." "I dare you to make five cold sales calls today." "I dare you to write five pages of your novel today."

- Take on a difficult problem that no one else wants to deal with. Not only will you win the respect and admiration of those who gave up on the problem, you will also increase your confidence in finding solutions to other problems. You may also find that you have discovered a niche no one else is covering—and an opportunity for you to make your mark.

- Start a joke collection. Nothing risqué or offensive, just light humor that makes you feel better. Pass on the jokes to friends and family; try to make someone else smile at least once every day.

NOTES